DISCARDED

A GREEN VELVET SECRET

A GREEN VELVET SECRET

Vicki Grant

tundra

Tundra Books, an imprint of Tundra Book Group, a division of Penguin
Random House of Canada Limited

Library and Archives Canada Cataloguing in Publication

Title: A green velvet secret / Vicki Grant.
Names: Grant, Vicki, author.
Identifiers: Canadiana (print) 20210351888 | Canadiana (ebook)
2021035190X | ISBN 9780735270121
  (hardcover) | ISBN 9780735270138 (EPUB)
Subjects: LCGFT: Novels.
Classification: LCC PS8613.R367 G74 2023 | DDC jC813/.6 — dc23

Published simultaneously in the United States of America by Tundra Books of
Northern New York, an imprint of Tundra Book Group, a division of Penguin
Random House of Canada Limited

Library of Congress Control Number: 2021949251

Edited by Lynne Missen.
Jacket designed by Sophie Paas-Lang.
The text was set in Adobe Caslon Pro.

Printed in Canada

www.penguinrandomhouse.ca

1 2 3 4 5   27 26 25 24 23

Penguin
Random House
TUNDRA BOOKS

tundra

For Colleen Kelly because, like Gidge,
she's shown how precious old friendships are.
And for Edwina Richardson because, like Yardley,
she would totally want the pantaloons.

WARNING!!!!

Bad things are going to happen in this book so be prepared.

Someone's going to die. Twice, in fact. (Or at least that's what it felt like to me.)

Other people are going to lie, cheat, steal, almost barf, break my heart and prance around in ridiculous outfits. (Normally, the ridiculous outfits wouldn't bother me unless, of course, it was my parents prancing around in them, which it was, so it did.)

I'm only warning you because I wish someone had warned *me*. But, ha! Like that was going to happen. Nothing Gidge loved better than surprises.

Except, I guess, me.

CHAPTER 1

Y ou'd never have known it from looking at her, what with the hair and the jewelry and everything, but Gidge was pretty practical. When she got the news, she just shrugged and went, "Bummer, man." She hugged everybody goodbye then jumped on her kick-scooter and headed to Scoops Dairy Bar for an organic key lime fro-yo to eat on the way home. By the time she'd turned onto our street she was hot, and her knees were making weird squeaking sounds, but she had a plan. She had to do three things. She got started right away.

Number One Thing: She took a spoon and began banging on this big old rusty triangle we have hanging next to the kitchen door. That's how you call a family meeting at our place. I was upstairs in my underwear, on my bed, happily bedazzling the denim skort I was planning to wear that day. I thought about pretending I hadn't heard the racket but *as if*. Gidge was really going at it.

I sighed and got up. I threw on another outfit — a flowered mini dress I'd bought for $3.29 at the Sally Ann, striped toe socks I'd won in a spelling bee and clunky pink sandals I'd dug out of the neighbor's garbage — then I went downstairs.

Mima and Pa were in the hall, blinking and scratching and making the kinds of sounds wounded animals make. "Dazed and confused" is the expression that comes to mind.

I clipped on my earrings and groaned. "What's this one about?"

I was sort of PO-ed. We'd already had one family meeting that week, and there's only so much brain-pickling boredom a girl can take. That meeting had been about bathroom rules and how some people weren't following them, by which I mean Pa. It wasn't the first time this had come up, but I was pretty sure we'd fixed the problem. The seat had been down ever since and there was always at least one square of toilet paper left on the roll for the next person. I couldn't think of anything else that had been an issue lately. People had been pretty good about the swear jar, taking the recycling out and not, like, *evaporating* when it was their turn to stir the compost (by which I also mean Pa, Pa and — loving but exasperated sigh — Pa).

I don't know why I thought my parents would be able to answer. They're basically out of it until they've had their first full bucket of coffee — and that's on a *good* day.

This was not a good day. They'd only managed to get a couple of hours sleep before Gidge started in with the clanging. They'd had a dress rehearsal the night before. Their play still stunk so they'd stayed really late at the theater trying to unstink it. They looked fried. They were both wearing plaid boxer shorts and baggy T-shirts for indie bands no one outside our family had ever heard of. Their faces were red and splotchy. Their hair was flat on one side and all Albert-Einstein-y on the other. They looked like really big, really cool toddlers just waking up from their naps.

"Huh?" they said, at more or less exactly the same time. (Mima and Pa do most things at more or less exactly the same time. It creeps strangers out.)

I didn't bother asking again. I figured I'd find out soon enough. Gidge was never one to hold back. I went to the kitchen. My parents shuffled along behind me.

I peeked around the door and gasped, although maybe just in my head. Usually, our kitchen's nothing fancy. Half our family meetings are about trying to find money to replace the counter where it's burnt or fix the ceiling where it's leaking or buy a fridge that actually keeps things on the cool side. But that day? Wow. HGTV or what? Silver balloons were tied to the backs of the kitchen chairs with twirly ribbons. The pot rack was covered in tiny twinkly lights. There was a white cloth on the table, four sparkly wine glasses on a sparkly tray and a giant bottle of champagne with little teardrops of, I don't know, *dew* or something creeping down the sides. Everything smelled of lavender oil and a little ylang-ylang too.

Gidge was big into saving the world so no way she'd normally have balloons, let alone put the lights on if it wasn't totally pitch-black out. The champagne was a retirement gift from her last class of students. She'd been saving it for "something momentous."

What could be momentous enough for twinkly lights and champagne at ten-thirty in the morning? Gidge believed in celebrating "all gifts from the universe" but I doubted even she'd go that crazy over a new fridge.

A few seconds later, she swanned into the kitchen from the backyard. (Even with the bad knees, Gidge tended to "swan.") She'd picked a bunch of white flowers from the garden. She put them in this brown clay vase Pa had made her when he was little. IMO, the vase looks exactly like a big fresh pile of dog poo, but she liked it.

She'd lined her eyes in smudgy black, so they looked super bright, like green Smarties or baby peas or something. She was wearing a purple silk caftan, massive chandelier earrings and a mittful of rings.

She placed the vase on the table and said, "Don't you just love lilies?"

Pa was leaning against the doorframe. He moaned and

went, "Sure. But not as much as I love sleep."

"Oh, now. You'll have plenty of time to sleep later. Sit. Sit. Sit," she said, and we did. She put on this big smile then looked at each of us, one at a time. She folded her hands on the table, closed her eyes, took a few deep breaths, then her face went all shiny. She said, "I called you here to announce that I'm starting an exciting new phase of my life."

I slapped my hands over my mouth. It might have looked like I was trying not to barf, but it was actually happiness I was holding in. My toes started tapping like I was getting ready to blast off into space, which I kind of was. Ever since she'd retired, Gidge had been working on her fashion portfolio. Just the week before, she'd finished final drawings for her entire winter collection. It was aimed at older women and featured clothes "as stylish, youthful and" — okay, *now* I'm trying not to barf — "sexy as you are." She called the collection "Now or Neverland," and it was, of course, fabulous. I'd helped her research companies online that might be interested in making her designs. We'd sent out a bunch of promotional packages. I figured she'd found a taker.

I wished I'd finished bedazzling my skort. I felt underdressed. This was a big deal.

"Gidge." I was so excited. "Is this? Um . . . Is it . . . ?"

She patted my hand. Her eyes twinkled. "It's cancer," she said. "Terminal cancer."

That's how my grandmother told us she was dying.

No, I thought. I shook my whole body like a dog coming out of a pond. *That's impossible. Gidge can't die. She wouldn't. Gidge isn't like that.* But then Pa and Mima clunked their heads on the table and started to sob and the world changed forever. I clunked my head on the table and started to sob too. Gidge swooped in and put her arms around us. The sleeves of her caftan fluttered over us like the wings of a fairy god-mother, which was no doubt exactly the look she'd been going for. She kissed our hair and laughed and kissed us some more then scrunched us all into a big group hug, which was sticky and awkward and smelled like someone hadn't brushed their teeth in a while.

"What a bunch of babies. We're all going to die! I'm one of the lucky ones. At least I get to know when. This is a gift, darlings! I've been given the chance to go out in my own perfect way."

Gidge opened the champagne. The cork popped and we all jumped as if she'd shot us, which she kind of had. Foam gushed out and fizzed down the sides. Nobody wanted any so Gidge made some stupid toast to the gods and slurped it up alone. She let us cry until we'd cried ourselves out, then she pushed the table to the side, cranked up the Rolling Stones and made us dance. It took a while, but she was right. It *did* make us feel better, by which I mean *a tiny bit*, and only as long as we danced hard enough not to remember why we were doing it. Our kitchen's small so we kept bumping into each other or stomping on each other's feet or getting thwacked in the face with Gidge's earrings or wizardly sleeves or crazy kinky white hair.

Maybe other people would have found that irritating, but I liked it. I liked being so close it hurt. It reminded me we were all still together.

CHAPTER 2

Number Two Thing Gidge had to do: get her karma in order. In case you don't know, karma is payback time, only from the universe. People like Gidge believe if you do bad stuff in this lifetime, you're going to be sorry in the next one. You'll come back as a dung beetle or a naked mole-rat or maybe even a human being again, only now you'll be covered in warts or allergic to sugar or addicted to blurting out inappropriate comments in class or something. That's what bad karma is, and Gidge didn't have much time left to fix hers.

The next day we were on the couch in the living room. It used to be maroon but it had gone kind of pink in places. That's where we always sat. I was leaning against her arm with my legs stretched out on the seat. Gidge was drinking orange juice with "just a splash" of leftover champagne in it. (More than a splash, if you asked me. I was worried this champagne-for-breakfast thing was going to become a habit.

Other than the fro-yo and the nose ring, Gidge had always been pretty careful about what she put in her body.)

She went, "Want to help me?"

"Duh," I said.

"That's a yes?"

"I *said* duh. Your ears broken or something?"

I didn't look up from the safety-pin necklace I was pretending to make. I was sort of mad at her, so no way I was going to be nice, but *of course* I wanted to help. Except when I was at school, Gidge and I did everything together — plus who else was going to help? She'd decided not to tell her friends until the very last minute because she didn't want them making a fuss. My parents practically begged to help her, but Gidge didn't want that either. She went, "Absolutely not! The summer season at the theater is starting in a few weeks. You've got enough on your plate. The show must go on — even if I can't."

When she said stuff like that, Mima and Pa "smiled bravely," because they were professional actors and could do that type of thing, but I had to go *la-la-la-la-la* in my head until she stopped. Gidge might have been thrilled she was dying but that didn't mean I had to be.

As for the bad karma, I figured it wouldn't take Gidge long to deal with it. I mean, even if she was sort of annoying at the moment, she was still the best person in the world ever. How much could there be to clean up?

I said, "How long's this going to take? A couple of hours or something? I'd kind of like to finish this necklace today."

"Oh, way longer than that! I might look like a harmless old lady, but I've done some wicked, wicked things. I've got to deal with them fast before the universe deals with me." She seemed almost sad for a second, but then she gave her head a jiggle and laughed. "So better get a move on, little darling. We've got work to do."

She sent me to the artists' co-op to buy a whole bunch of these special handmade note cards. I didn't know what the big whoop about them was. To me, they looked like wet Kleenex someone had squished flat and folded, but Gidge liked them. By the time I got back from the store, she'd set up a rickety little table in the sunny part of the yard and plunked her old typewriter on it. She'd picked fresh flowers for Pa's poo vase and put her favorite cushion on her folding chair to keep her back from hurting.

"Now what?" I said.

Gidge slipped a card into the typewriter and rolled it into place. "I'm going to write some long-overdue letters and you're going to weed the garden. Also long overdue." She tried to tell me weeding was part of the karma thing too, but I'm pretty sure it was just a chore. She said I could clean the fridge instead if I wanted — like *that* was going to make the universe happy — but I said no. At least I'd be near her out here. I changed into a weeding outfit — white crop top, green rubber boots with frog eyes on the toes and silver lamé overalls from this goofy play my parents did called *Disco Doppelgangers* — and got to work.

I tried to talk with Gidge while I weeded, but every time I said something she'd just go, "Huh? Sorry, darling. What?" and then not even listen when I said it again. Sooo irritating. Pretty soon I gave up. What was the use? She was, like, *obsessed* with getting those letters written. When Gidge got it in her head to do something, even I couldn't get through to her.

I kept weeding away but mostly I just watched her. I watched Gidge a lot, now that I knew I wouldn't be able to forever. After a while, I noticed she started all the letters the same way. She'd tilt her head and get this weird zombie look on her face as if some giant vacuum cleaner was sucking her spirit out through her ear. She'd stay like that for a really long time, then, just when I was ready to run screaming for help, she'd raise her hands in the air like some fancy piano player and slam them down on the keyboard. She'd type away like crazy until she was done, then she'd tear the card out of the typewriter. She'd settle back in her chair, all chill and Zen and Gidge again, and read it over. Every so often I'd hear her chuckle, or sniffle, or swear but that was usually in a good way, as if she was just so *amazed* at how brilliant she was. (I still made her put money in the swear jar.) Once she was finished, she'd type the address onto the envelope, slip in the card and seal it with a big, red, lipstick-y kiss.

After a couple of hours of weeding, I'd had enough. My fingers were all cut up from the thorns and I was pretty sure I had actual ants in my actual pants. I got up and smacked the dirt off my hands.

Gidge must have written about fifteen cards by then. I picked up the top one. "Can I read it?"

"No." She grabbed it back from me.

"How about this one then?" I squinted at the address. "Who's Mrs. M. —"

Her hand kaboomed down on the pile before I got any farther. "No," she said. "You're not reading any of them."

"What? How come?" We never kept secrets from each other. Or at least I didn't think we did. (Boy, was I wrong.)

"It's my karma, not yours. So, shoo." She winked, but she meant it.

"Oh, come on."

"Nu-uh."

"At least tell me what's in them."

She flicked her hand and went, "Nothinnng," all long and drawn out and chuckle-ish as if I was being silly, which was also weird. Gidge had always been pretty good about not treating me like a child.

"Pants on fire," I said.

She squinted up one eye like *who you callin' a liar?* but then she laughed. "Fine. You caught me. Clearly there'd be no point in sending letters with nothing in them, now, would there? Okay,

Let me see . . . Recipes, poems, abject apologies, predictions, cleaning tips, jokes . . . that type of thing." She put her elbows over the cards and tapped her fingers on the table. "Happy?"

I folded my arms and said, "Pants still smoking," because that didn't sound like a "type of thing" to me. It sounded like several completely different types of things, some *way* more interesting than others.

I tried to weasel some details out of her, but she said, "Oh, *now* you're just being nosy," and sent me out to buy stamps. "Pretty ones," she said, as if she had to tell me that.

By the time I got back from the post office, she'd put the letters in two different piles. She said the first pile was to mail right away. The other pile was to go out "after I do."

"La-la-la-la-la-la-la," I said out loud.

Gidge laughed and said, "You do so hear me."

She stuck stamps on the first bunch of letters and got me to drop them in the mailbox. She wrote dates on Post-it notes and stuck them on the other letters, then she wrapped them all up in crinkly brown paper and a polka-dot ribbon she'd saved from my birthday. She gave that pile to Pa when he got home and told him to pay special attention to the dates the letters were supposed to be mailed on.

He opened his mouth really wide and huffed out this big fake sigh. "Are you planning to keep running our lives from the grave?"

"Of course I am!" She laughed and kissed his forehead.

I thought she was joking but she wasn't.

CHAPTER 3

Gidge was still pretty energetic so, for a while there, we spent almost all our time on karma patrol. KP duty, she called it. Some of it was so boring you wouldn't believe, like canceling her magazine subscriptions or going through filing cabinets in the attic or organizing all her passwords so Mima and Pa would know how to access her accounts "when the time comes." (*La-la-la-la-la-la.*)

Other stuff, though, was major fun. Gidge always used to say, "Nothing's better for your karma than making other people happy," so we did a lot of that. We dug up big bunches of Gidge's lilies, put on our cutest camo gear, then snuck out in the middle of the night and planted them in places that could use some love. Empty-chip-bag-and-cat-pee kind of places. Bus shelters with broken glass and dirty words. Houses with boarded-up windows. The icky patch just outside the hospital where patients with tubes sticking out of them sit in their wheelchairs smoking. Someday, there'll be beautiful flowers poking up through the cigarette butts, and those people won't know it but it'll be Gidge making them feel just a little bit better.

Then there was this one lunchtime we set ourselves up on a park bench downtown and gave away most of Gidge's earrings. It was all just stuff we'd churned out during our beading phase but it made people feel good. Didn't matter who it was — skater kids, homeless guys, businesspeople who tried to tell us they were too busy to stop — everybody laughed and smiled and tucked their hair behind their ears to take a selfie in their fabulous new jewelry. They all wanted to hug Gidge, but I made them hug me instead even though I'm not really crazy about strangers. I didn't want them giving Gidge their germs. She'd had a round of chemotherapy by then. Chemotherapy, if you don't know, is when they put poison in your veins to try and kill the cancer. But, like, *major fail*. I'm pretty sure all it did was make the cancer stronger and Gidge weaker. Even *I* had to wash my hands before I hugged her now.

Usually, it was pretty easy to forget Gidge was dying because she didn't seem any different. By which I mean her *brain* didn't. She still did all the normal things. She laughed and danced and got dressed up and bossed us around and regularly made us stop whatever we were doing to marvel at some random "miracle of the cosmos."

There was only one time I remember her being really un-Gidge-y. It was a Friday, a couple of weeks before school ended. Teachers had a PD day so I was home, hanging out with Gidge. The mail had just come flying through the slot in the front door. She scurried over to get it, all twittery and excited as if this was Christmas or something even though the mail comes five times a week so it's really not that big a deal. She flipped through the pile of envelopes and her face went sad.

"What?" I hated her sad face.

"Nothing," she said, which she was saying way too often these days. I squinted at her hard, but she still didn't answer so I went, "What?" again.

Her lips moved around her face as if she was trying to come up with some reason not to tell me.

"Gidggggggggge," I said, like a plane taking off.

She sighed and showed me the orange sticker slapped onto one of the envelopes.

"'Return to sender'?" I read. "What does that mean?"

"It means 'send this back to the person who wrote it.' The post office puts that on letters they can't deliver."

"Why couldn't they deliver it?"

"Oh, well . . ." She shoved the envelope into her bra and turned away. "I was too late, I guess."

I wanted to ask *Too late for what?* but didn't. Lots of Gidge's friends were old. Lots of them were dying. I figured that's what must have happened to this person. Making Gidge say it out loud would just have made her sadder.

In other words, I was being nice — but she must have missed that. She spun around and pointed her finger at me. "So don't you save your 'sorry's for later. You hear me? You might miss your chance."

I was like, "*Whoa.* Wha'd I do? Who do *I* have to apologize to? I'm twelve! Do you think I don't have time to —"

"Doesn't matter. Don't keep an apology to yourself. When you make a mistake, say sorry or you'll *be* sorry — that's what I'm telling you. I have one regret and it's that I didn't do it myself when I had the chance."

It was scary, the way she said it. Not like woo-woo-monster-scary, more like who-*is*-this-person-scary. The happy stuff in her eyes had totally disappeared and now all that was left was old. And after old comes dead. That's what scared me.

"I will," I said. "I promise."

She said, "Good," but she turned away from me so I couldn't see her face. I put my arms around her stomach and leaned my cheek against her back. She patted my hand. I could hear her heart pounding.

I said, "Want to go to The Pit of Despair?"

CHAPTER 4

The Pit of Despair was Gidge's name for this old deserted gravel quarry just outside the city. It was her secret place. She'd gone there ever since she was a kid, and sometimes she took me. It was just a big giant hole, the kind a meteor would make if it crashed into Earth at top speed. There were no trees or anything around it. Just dirt and mud and rocks and one rickety little jelly bean of a camper-trailer with a broken window that a raggedy yellow curtain fluttered out of when the wind blew. Everything about The Pit of Despair looked unloved and ugly and hopeless. "It looks the way sad feels," Gidge used to say. That's why she liked it.

She'd save up all the rotten things in her life then take them to The Pit of Despair. Sometimes she'd bring chalk and write bad stuff on the rocks, just to get it out of her system. She didn't have to feel guilty about what she wrote because there was no one around other than me to see it, and the rain would wash it off sooner or later anyway.

Other times, she'd just sit dangling her legs over the edge of the Pit. She'd sit there with her problems until they got "on friendlier terms again." That's what she used to say. I didn't think cancer was the type of thing you'd ever want to get friendly with, but Gidge claimed the Pit could do magic. A couple hours there and a fro-yo on the way home and she'd be good as new again.

But when the letter got returned-to-sender and I asked her if she wanted to go to the Pit, she just laughed. She said, "Oh, no, darling. Much as I love a good wallow, no time for that now! Too much to do before I'm past my best-before date. Speaking of which . . ." She waggled her eyebrows. "Can I interest you in a little excursion of a different kind?"

I never said no to an excursion, especially if it was good enough for an eyebrow-waggle. "Where to?"

She grabbed handfuls of her hair and scrunched them in her fists. (Gidge always scrunched before we went some-where special. It kept the curls in.) "Gates of Heaven Cemetery," she said.

"Ce-me-ter-y?" I sort of smiled. It wasn't exactly what I'd had in mind, but she looked so thrilled I tried to stay positive.

"Yes ma'am." More scrunching. "I've got an old friend there who'll know how to fix my little problem with the letter. I can hardly wait for you to meet her!"

Gidge bustled off to pack some stuff. I went to my room and tried to figure out what to wear to a graveyard. By the time I was dressed, Gidge was at the front door, all lipstick-ed up and ready to go.

We took the number 42 bus to the end of the line then got on our scooters. We didn't get very far. Every couple of minutes Gidge would go, "Why don't we sit for a moment and contemplate the view?" which was exactly the type of thing Gidge *would* say if we were on a mountain or by a lake or even downtown when all the Christmas lights were up, but now we were leaning on a hot metal railing beside a dumpster or a used car lot or a sign that read "Warning: Falling Rocks."

I knew better than to ask if she was feeling all right. Gidge absolutely *loved* talking about dying, except of course the part about how much it hurt.

She sat there beside the highway panting and gasping and pretending to smile. I was pretty sure it wouldn't be long before she went, "Okay. Up and at it!" as if she was just rarin' to go again, which she totally wasn't. Knowing Gidge, she'd just keep trudging along until she collapsed, and then we'd both be in trouble. She was smaller than she used to be but still way too big for me to carry.

So I said, "Want to hitchhike?" Normally I'd never even have considered it, what with all the homicidal maniacs out there and everything, but I was desperate.

"Hitchhike? Now you're talkin'!" Gidge jumped up as if her knees still worked and stuck out her thumb.

A car went past without even slowing down, so she lifted her skirt up to her thigh like she was showing off her legs, which is a joke all old ladies pull any time you say the word *hitchhike*. A white-haired guy in mirrored sunglasses and a red convertible was heading the other way but I guess he liked Gidge's legs or felt sorry for us or something, because he hung a U-ey and swung back to pick us up.

"Well, whaddya know?" Gidge gave a little wiggle. "Looks like the old girl's still got it!" She practically danced over to the car. I folded up our scooters and ran after her.

CHAPTER 5

Barry — that was the guy's name — dropped us at the front entrance of Gates of Heaven and we went in. If you've only seen cemeteries in cartoons, you kind of expect them to be dark and cloudy with ghosts squiggling up from the headstones like smoke from a toaster, but this one wasn't like that. It had really green grass and trees shaped like giant pieces of broccoli and swoopy paths that made me want to get back on my scooter. If you didn't mind dead people, it would have been the perfect place for a picnic. (I felt a little silly dressed entirely in black lace, although I did still like the look. Even Barry had complimented my veil.)

We had a map of the cemetery but it still took us forever to find Gidge's friend who just so happened to be dead. (If you'd known Gidge that wouldn't surprise you.) When we finally found the grave, Gidge was pale and shaky and had little diamonds of sweat in her hair. She patted her face with a hankie and went, "Whoo. Warm day," even though it wasn't really. She rummaged around in her big straw bag and pulled out a Mickey Mouse Pez dispenser, a half-empty bottle of rum and a ratty pair of sandals made from old tire treads. She arranged them on the grave like some weird little art project, sprinkled everything with sage oil, then mumbled something. I thought it was a prayer at first or maybe a magical incantation, but she laughed too hard at the end for that. Might have been a dirty joke.

She sat down beside the grave and smiled at it. She didn't actually say anything, but you'd have sworn she was having a conversation with it. She nodded. Laughed. Looked up at the sky to think about something the dead person must have said, then nodded again. She even got a pen out of her bag and took a couple notes in the little scribbler she always kept with her.

After a while, as in *forever*, I said, "You done here?" I was getting bored.

"Yup. Got my marching orders." She kissed the tips of her fingers, then touched the gravestone and said to it, "Thank you, darling. I feel so much better! In your own crazy way, you always were incredibly wise."

Maybe I was jealous, but I didn't like the look on her face. I went, "What's so great about Carole-Anne Libitzki?" That was the name carved into the stone.

Gidge laughed and struggled up to her feet. "Carole-Anne. Wow. I almost forgot that was her real name." She shook her head. "Man. She was *so* not a Carole-Anne."

"What was she then?"

"A KooKoo. That's what everyone called her. Such an amazing spirit." She smiled at the gravestone again and said, "We had some fun, didn't we, Kooks?"

Then she turned to me. "I wish you had someone like KooKoo in your life. A best friend. Someone to talk to . . . laugh with . . . trust with all your important secrets."

"I do," I said, and I nuzzled my head into her armpit.

"Someone your own age, I mean."

I pulled away and looked at her. The chemo must have been eating her brain. Gidge never said stuff like that. Whenever my parents or teachers brought up the whole "lonely" thing, she always went, "Pff. Yardley's fine. She's happy. She'll find her tribe one of these days." She didn't know what the fuss was about and neither did I. It's not like I was an outcast or anything. It's not like other kids at school were mean to me. They thought I was a bit on the weird side but, hey, that's fair, and anyway, I thought they were a bit on the boring side. (Also fair.) They asked me to parties and stuff. I just didn't want to go. We didn't have anything in common.

Not like Gidge and me. We had everything in common.

We loved crafting, guerrilla fashion and unexpected color combinations. We strongly disliked branded athleisure wear and throwaway clothes. We were even both highly allergic to cats. (I had a T-shirt once with a picture of a cat on it and even *that* made me feel like sneezing.) "Two peas in a stylish little pod," Pa used to say.

I said to Gidge, "I don't need anyone else."

"But you will. And maybe sooner than you think. The problem with spending all your time with adults is that they —"

"Stop."

"If I knew you had a KooKoo to take my place, I'd —"

"Stop."

"But a friend would —"

"Gidge! I don't want a friend."

"But maybe you need one. Plus you're too fabulous not to share with the world. I'm going to be gone soon and I'd hate to think you —"

I said, "La-la-la-la-la-la-la" *really* loud and kept saying it until she got the hint. Gidge and her stupid matchmaking. That's what this was. At the time, I didn't know what she was up to — or all the problems it was going to cause me. I was just mad she was talking about dying again.

Gidge gave an upside-down smile and tweaked my nose, then her face went funny and she had to sit down on KooKoo again.

I knew that look. She was getting a pain. She leaned against the headstone, opened the bottle of rum and took a sip, by which I mean a *gulp*.

"Sorry, Kooks," she said, "but I'm pretty sure I need this more than you do." Is there a word for laughing with your mouth but crying with your eyes? If there is, that's what Gidge was doing.

She wagged her finger at me. "Before you say anything, these are happy tears." She dabbed her face with the hankie again. "For time well wasted."

She smiled, and I believed her. I snuggled down next to her.

After a while she said, "Take a look at this, would you?" She spread out her arm like she was a spokesmodel on a game show and the cemetery was the grand prize. "Lovely, isn't it?"

I nodded. It was pretty.

"KooKoo's final resting place. Do you know that's what people used to call graves? The final resting place." She let out a big loud "Ha!" and then coughed and coughed and coughed and had to have another sip of rum before she could keep going. "As if the spirit would ever rest! It's only the body that gives up. At death, the spirit shrugs off its mortal remains then runs around naked and free until it finds a new home."

"Ick," I said.

"Sounds pretty good to me." She tipped her head back against the stone and took a few deep breaths. Some birds chirped. The wind made the leaves on the trees flutter. The clouds looked like whipped cream and the sky like blue highlighter. I thought about making a shirt that color some day.

"Such a shame they chose this place," Gidge said. "They clearly didn't know her. Why would they have buried her body here?"

"Who?"

"KooKoo's parents. They were the type of people who actually believed in final resting places. Why would they ever think KooKoo would want to spend all eternity *here*?"

"I thought you said it was lovely. I thought you said the spirit doesn't rest."

"I did. And it doesn't. But still. Not much of a send-off, is it? KooKoo wouldn't want lovely! She was dramatic. Extravagant. A bird of paradise! If ever there was someone who should have gone out with a bang, it was her."

"What do you think they should have done, then?"

"Something fun, like . . . I dunno . . . turned her cremated remains into finger paint . . . or fireworks or, or . . . shot them off the top of a roller coaster with water guns!"

I laughed.

"Don't laugh. People do that."

"Seriously?"

"Better than seriously. They do it joyously! Can you imagine anything better than that?"

Yeah. Not dying at all, I thought.

Gidge looked at the sky and smiled. "Hmm . . . I like that idea. Being shot off a roller coaster. What a beautiful way to be returned to Mother Earth! I love the thought of all the people down below putting their hands out and going, 'I feel rain,' not knowing that it's pure love and happiness sprinkling down on them."

Again — *ick*. But I didn't want to ruin the mood, so I was like, *Yeah, spray the world with dead bodies. Great idea!*

Gidge closed her eyes and nodded. "I think that's the way I'd like to go."

I sat up. "Really?"

She thought about it for a second. "Yeah. Kooks and I had some great times at the harborfront amusement park — plus I like roller coasters, the whole idea of them. The ups, the downs. The laughter, the screaming. The way you feel absolute terror at the exact same moment you're thinking you've never had so much fun ever. That's what life's all about, isn't it? That joyful, terrifying mix."

She looked at me as if I'd know, which I didn't. Sometimes I think she forgot I was twelve.

"Yup," she said. "That's what I'd want to do. Be shot off the top of the harborfront roller coaster. That is, if I hadn't already decided to donate my body to science." She shrugged. "Oh well. Maybe if the med school has any leftovers, you could use those."

"Gidge!" I covered my ears. "Would you stop saying stuff like that?"

"Oh, now, now, now, now, now." Gidge put her arm around me and rocked back and forth. "Don't you worry. Death doesn't scare me. I'm excited about what fabulous experience the universe has waiting for me. What new life I'll take on when I leave this one behind."

"Gidge!"

"Sorry, sorry!" She drew her fingers across her lips like she was zipping them closed.

We sat like that for a while, all snuggly and quiet and alive, then she said, "Okay, help me up and let's get going. Not a good idea to get too comfortable here. Despite what I may look like, I'm not quite ready for the grave. I still have things on my to-do list!"

I stood up. She held out her hand and I pulled. It wouldn't have taken much to yank her arm right out of the socket, that's how skinny she was. It gave me the creeps. Gidge was like a snowman. She'd started out kind of plump and jolly and now she was melting away before my eyes. I suddenly imagined waking up one day and finding nothing left but a puddle, two bright green pebbles and a carrot with a nose ring.

I shook the picture out of my head. I had to stop thinking that way. We had to just keep working, working, working as hard as we could to clean up her karma. If we did it right, maybe someday I'd get a budgie or a puppy or a new next-door neighbor and I'd realize Gidge had come back to me, better than ever.

I got her onto her feet, dusted the dirt off her bum and scrunched her hair up the way she liked it. We took a bunch of selfies with KooKoo, then we headed home.

Gidge had to lean on my shoulder when we went up the hill. The guy who'd been mowing the cemetery lawn saw us and offered to drive us to the bus stop.

"I was going that way anyway," he said.

That was the funny thing about Gidge. People always seemed to be going the way she needed to go.

CHAPTER 6

The trip to the cemetery took a lot out of Gidge, or maybe it was the rum. The next day she could hardly get out of bed.

"Perfect!" she said, as if she'd planned it that way all along. "I'll just laze about like the Queen of Sheba and you can clean out my closet for me."

Gidge claimed cleaning the closet was all about karma too, but it just sounded like another chore to me. At least it was one I liked. Gidge used to be the costume design teacher at Chedabucto High School of the Arts. She made all her own clothes, and they were awesome. She kept a lot of them in this giant curlicue closety-thing she'd found on the side of the road when someone tore down an old house. We called it "The Wardrobe Department." That's how big it was.

That afternoon, Gidge sat on her bed, propped up by a pile of sparkly cushions. I don't know about Sheba, but Gidge sure looked like the Queen of Something. I brought her green tea in her favorite mug and put a crazy quilt over her legs to keep her from getting a chill, then I pretended I was some lowly minion working at a fancy dress shop and she was some really rich lady. I pulled things out of the closet one at a time and draped them over my arm for her to inspect. Gidge put on a bad French accent and pretended to boss me around.

"Oof!" she'd go, if she wanted me to throw something right in the Salvation Army bag.

If she went "Unh!" and flicked her hand at me, it meant she wanted it to go to Mima.

I really hated it when she did that. At least with the Salvation Army pile someone would actually *wear* the clothes. Mima didn't care about fashion. We both knew she was just going to chop up anything Gidge gave her and turn it into a wall hanging for the so-called lobby of the theater. I found that too painful to even *contemplate* — but it didn't faze Gidge. She'd gotten so weird. She'd held onto all her precious clothes forever, but now it was like, "Off with their heads!"

My favorite reaction was when I pulled this floaty hippie-angel-princess dress out of The Wardrobe Department and Gidge went, "Oooooooh," all long and swoopy. I knew I'd hit the jackpot. I squee-ed and jumped onto the bed.

"I forgot about this!" Gidge dropped the French accent and picked up the dress. "I wore it opening night of the Deep Roots Folk Festival in '69. Or maybe '70? Oh, who cares?

Ancient history. Anyway . . . I had absolutely no money, but I wanted to look fabulous, so I went to the Army Surplus store and bought ten dollars' worth of World War Two parachute silk. That's what I made it out of."

She suddenly pointed at me as if I'd done something wrong. "Don't forget to give yourself a little treat when you have the chance. It's important, and you deserve it." She was always doing that now. Stopping right in the middle of a perfectly good story to give me another life lesson.

She smiled. "Anyway . . . it's kind of lovely, isn't it? The cap sleeves and the smocking at the bodice . . . Oh, and would you look at that!" She put on her reading glasses and we both squinted at the tiny, perfect daisy chain embroidered around the hem. "You know, YaYa, it's the little things that make all the difference." I had a feeling that was a life lesson, too.

She told me she used to wear the dress with rings on her toes and wildflowers in her hair. Back then, she lived in a falling-down mansion with some friends and a parrot called J. Alfred Prufrock who she'd taught to say, "Darling, I *love* your outfit!" whenever she walked in the room. Up until she told me that story, I'd thought I knew everything there was to know about Gidge, but I didn't. (Like really, *really* didn't, but I'm getting to that.)

"Can I try it on?" I said.

She smiled over her teacup. "I'd be devastated if you didn't."

I stripped down to my undies and pulled the dress over my head. Gidge used to be taller than me. The hem swirled around my feet like soft-serve ice cream. She also must have had some major boobage happening because the top of the dress didn't fit me very well either, but it was still really pretty. I gave a little twirl and checked myself out in the full-length mirror.

"Can I keep it?" I said.

"No. Sorry, darling. That's going to the consignment shop."

"The what?"

"The consignment shop. It's a place where people take their clothes to sell."

"*Sell?*" I said, like I'd never heard the word before. How could she sell something as beautiful as this?

She nodded and smiled.

I pleaded. I begged. I tried to talk her out of it. I'd rather have kept all Gidge's stuff and starved to death than sell it to someone who didn't love her. But Gidge wouldn't listen. She'd been worried about how we were going to survive after she was gone. She'd talked about it a lot in our family meetings. She was leaving us the house and some savings but that's all she had. Her pension "died with her." (*La-la-la-la-la-la-la.*) She always ended the meetings by hugging us and kissing us and saying, "But who needs money when you've got love, right?"

Nobody ever answered, at least not out loud. People with no business sense who run weird little independent theaters need money, that's who. Even I know that. Gidge used to say, "We aren't very practical, but we sure do have fun!" She didn't say that anymore.

I took off the dress and put my own outfit back on, which I used to like but didn't now. It was like eating dessert before you've had your vegetables. You might love brussels sprouts but they're still going to taste terrible after double-fudge brownies. I put a smile on my face and went back to cleaning out the closet. I hoped karma was watching.

That afternoon, we found quite a few clothes that made Gidge go "Ooooh!" — especially a pair of yellow crocheted hot pants with matching patent-leather go-go boots. (Those got a double "Ooooh!" from me.) I didn't try any of them on. Why torture myself? It was all going to be sold.

While Gidge had a nap, I looked up consignment stores online. The day after school ended, we wrapped her most valuable clothes in recycled dry cleaner bags and took the bus downtown.

CHAPTER 7

We started at a shop called Over Easy Vintage Emporium. It was on a street where the good shops used to be when Gidge was young, but now it was just kind of skeevy. The stores all had "Going Out of Business" signs in their windows or sold weird stuff like vacuum cleaner attachments or secondhand photocopiers or nighties that had holes in all the wrong places. (And I'm talking *all* the wrong places. The places normal people try to cover up, if you know what I mean.)

Over Easy really stood out. The building was old, but the paint was new and blue as a swimming pool. There was a neon sign squeaking on a pole over the door. The whole place looked like it belonged in one of those old movies where the actors wear hats and smoke a lot. We stood on the sidewalk for a moment checking out the window display. A manne-quin in a ruby red suit with giant shoulders and a tiny waist was holding a cocktail glass with a little umbrella in it. We squinted to see the price tag on the suit.

"Ooh. A hundred and fifty bucks!" Gidge nudged me. We bit our lips and bugged our eyes out at each other. That was a lot of money. "I think we'll do quite well here, don't you?"

I nodded. She scrunched her hair, and we went inside.

A bell tinkled when we opened the door. It was cool in the shop, but the air, I don't know, smelled *cozy* or something. We looked around. The floor was red-and-black checkerboard. The cash register was gold and fancy and sitting on a big, thick, shiny wooden counter. The wall behind it had shelves going right up to the ceiling, all stacked with flat cardboard boxes labeled "Ecru Silk, Ladies Medium" and "Dusty Rose, High-Waisted" and other equally fabulous word-pictures normally only found in my head. Another wall was covered with posters for pillbox hats and old-fashioned vanishing cream and seriously pointy bras.

There were mannequins everywhere, too. Only a few of them had legs, but they all had long necks, red lips and eyebrows so skinny they looked like they'd been drawn on with a Sharpie. They were posed with their arms down straight and their hands bent up and their heads turned away as if they knew exactly how hot they were compared to the rest of us. There was a giant mirror in the corner and I could see almost the whole shop in it.

Gidge sighed. "I just died and went to heaven." I didn't even *think* of going *la-la-la*. I knew exactly how she felt.

A boy was sitting in a chair at the back of the store. His name was Harris, but I didn't know that then, or how bad he was going to mess things up for me, either. I remember thinking he didn't look like anything special. Flip-flops, shorts, glasses, ballcap. I was more interested in the chair. It was old but kind of space-age too, as if it had been designed a hundred years ago by someone imagining what the future was going to be like. I kind of loved it. "A genuine Barcalounger," Gidge whispered when she saw me looking. "Such a period piece."

I was pretty sure the boy didn't care what kind of chair he was sitting on or what we thought about it. He had his face in a puzzle book and was scribbling away as if the teacher had just walked in and he had homework to finish. On the floor beside the chair were four more books just like the one he was holding. They were as fat as *Harry Potter and the Order of the Phoenix*, only taller and made out of the type of paper coloring books are. The kind of books you usually only see beside toilets.

Gidge went, "Why, hello there!" as if she was positively *delighted* to make his acquaintance.

He didn't look up. He just hollered, "Connie!" so loud Gidge and I jumped like cartoon rabbits.

A thin guy in a snappy gray suit beetled through a door marked "Office" at the back of the shop. "Sorry, sorry! Didn't hear you come in. I just got a new order of the most spectacular —"

He stopped dead. He spread his hand over his skinny tie and gawked at us for a second, then he went, "Ms. O'Hanlon?!" and charged at Gidge. He threw his arms around her and squeezed, and I mean like *hard*, as if he was trying to get the last bit of toothpaste out of her or something.

I was thinking *Germs!* or maybe *Crazy person!* but Gidge was smiling her face off. She went, "Conrad Kim," and her voice was so happy there was no way I was going to break this up, even if he turned out to have rabies or something. They kept hugging and stepping back to look at each other and then hugging some more.

The boy put down his puzzle book and turned to see what all the commotion was about.

I gave him one of those awkward smiles and whispered, "I know!" as in *Ugh. Adults.* He didn't have to laugh, but he could have at least smiled back.

But did he?

No. He turned away as if I had a nose booger and went back to his book.

I checked out a rack of summer dresses and waited for Gidge to remember I was there.

I found out — as in *eventually* — that Conrad had been one of Gidge's best students. They hadn't seen each other since he'd graduated from high school twenty years ago.

"I knew there was a reason I walked in this door!" she said when they finally let go of each other. Con shooed the boy out of the chair so Gidge could sit down. "I thought you were out west," she said.

"I was. Had a big fancy job and the condo to match but . . ." Con shrugged. "You know how it is. My parents were delighted with the way my life was going, but I wasn't. Then my father got sick and they had to go into assisted living. My sister was having family problems and needed help, so I packed everything up, came home and opened Over Easy."

"And . . . ?"

"Couldn't be happier."

"Oh, I'm so pleased. I remember hearing you were off to university to take accounting and my heart just sank for you. After all our conversations! *So* not your thing, darling! You were always too good a boy, Conrad. That was your problem."

Gidge introduced me to Con ("My beloved granddaughter!") and Con introduced Harris to Gidge ("My beloved nephew!") and then they spent a few minutes being absolutely thrilled by the amazing coincidence that we were the same age.

"Twelve! Wow." Gidge made her mouth into a perfect O and shook her head.

"Both of them!" Con said. They looked back and forth at us, big grins on their faces. "Well, won't they have fun!"

I felt like when I was six and my parents went and arranged a playdate with some rando kid who just happened to be on the monkey bars at the same time I was. From then on, they always referred to him as "your friend Milo," and I'd always be like, "Who?" Did I really have to pretend we were friends? It just made me feel defective.

This time, though, I smiled. Not a big smile but polite. I was collecting karma points. I didn't know how many I'd need to keep Gidge from dying so I wasn't missing any opportunity. Harris, on the other hand, listened to them talk for about three seconds then just up and left. We all turned and watched him walk into Con's office and shut the door.

Awkward silence — then Con leaned toward us and whispered, "Excuse him. He's a great kid. He's just shy. He's having a bit of a rough time these days. I'll have a word with him about it later."

"No, no, that's okay," I said.

"It is not. It's rude!"

"I don't mind. Really." Mind? Ha! I was *thrilled* he'd left. I thought it meant I wouldn't have to bother about him anymore but, of course, I was wrong. The bothering was just about to start.

CHAPTER 8

Gidge and I ended up staying at Over Easy the whole afternoon. She told Con all about "this exciting new phase" of her life. Con hugged her some more — *he* clearly didn't think "exciting" was the right word either — then he gave us a tour of Over Easy.

We went through everything in the shop, piece by perfect piece. Gidge kept having to remind me to breathe. We were looking at an awesome buckskin maxi skirt with a fringed hem when Con mentioned he was getting a lot of interest in hippie stuff from the late sixties. So, that night, Gidge and I went through her closet again.

Next day, we went back to the shop with a bag full of lace halter tops, purple velvet bell-bottoms and crop-top peasant blouses. Harris tried to take off as soon as we showed up, but Con whumped his hand down onto his shoulder and went, "Whoa there, cowpoke. Where do you think you're going? Your friend's here." Harris went all splotchy and turned away.

Your friend.

Oh, the mortification.

I was Harris's Milo.

I shrugged and gave Con an embarrassed little smile. Con squeezed my arm like I was a good kid, then said, "Well, let's see what you've got here!"

He opened the bag and pretty soon Con was the one having trouble breathing.

He took everything we'd brought and sold it in days. Then he mentioned that eighties office-wear, oversized accessories and vintage high-waisted trousers were making a comeback too. Gidge was like: check, check, check.

We started going to Over Easy two or three times a week. Usually we had stuff to sell, but sometimes we went just because it made Gidge happy. Harris had stopped trying to escape when we showed up, but he pretty much avoided me. He found a spot in the corner and did his puzzles. Gidge and I would help Con redo the window display, or reorganize the shelves, or give clients a hand pulling an outfit together. When she'd get tired, she'd sit in the Barcalounger and read the newspaper or go into Con's office and write some more goodbye letters. She kept a big stack of those squished-Kleenex cards there, and Con didn't mind if she used his old

Remington typewriter. She'd drop the cards in the mailbox on our way home. A few envelopes were still coming back stamped "Return to Sender" but it didn't seem to bother her. She just kept writing new ones. Gidge was stubborn.

Meanwhile, the money was beginning to add up. One night, we dumped it all out on Gidge's bed and it came to $1,573. "At this rate," she said, "we'll have enough for you to go to camp next summer!"

I thought she was joking — I mean, I would absolutely *hate* camp and she knew it — but when I looked at her, I saw her smile had gone sort of wobbly and her eyebrows were cranked way up into the wouldn't-that-be-fabulous-? zone, and I realized she was back on the whole stupid KooKoo thing again. It was her new obsession. Finding me a friend. "A replacement," she said once, as if I could just trade her in for a newer model and everything would be good as new.

"Camp," I said. "Ugh." I put my finger down my throat in case she didn't get my point.

"Well, now. You don't know that. It could be —"

"Gross. Not *could* be. *Would* be. And I *do* know that."

"Lots of camps have art classes and —"

"Gidge!" I didn't like to scream at her, but seriously. There are laws against torturing small helpless animals such as myself.

She laughed as if she'd only been joking, then she changed

the subject and we started getting another bunch of clothes together for Con. By now, we'd gone through the entire Wardrobe Department and had moved on to rummaging through old trunks she'd stored away in the attic years ago and totally forgotten about. We found some major treasures — *Hello, bronze taffeta ballgown with matching rhinestone-encrusted bolero!* — but then we had to stop. Gidge couldn't make it upstairs anymore. Her pains had started getting worse. The doctors decided another round of chemo might make her more comfortable.

In case you don't know, "comfortable" is a bad thing. It's what doctors try to make you when they can't make you better.

CHAPTER 9

I went to the hospital with Gidge for her first few sessions of chemo. You'd think a cancer hospital would be horrible, but I liked it there.

We made friends with the other chemo patients. There was Edgar and Chibundu and Shelley and Sheila — I could never remember which was which — and Kwan and Dave and this teenage guy named Justin. They were all pretty cheery, even Justin, who looked exactly like Jack Skellington in *Nightmare Before Christmas*. That's how skinny and pale and bald he was from the chemo. Everybody sat in big La-Z-Boy chairs with the footrests up and plastic trays across their laps and see-through bags on rolly-poles dripping chemo into their arms. People played cards or watched TV or just blabbed away with each other. The best thing was that someone always showed up with a big plate of doughnuts or homemade cookies to share and nobody ever said, "Oh, I shouldn't!" or "I'm cutting back on sugar" or "Caramel sticks to my fillings." (Gidge used to say her favorite thing about cancer was how it made people stop worrying about stupid stuff.)

So like I said, I was happy at the hospital, but that didn't matter. Our third day there Gidge just up and decided I wasn't allowed to come anymore. She told me so right after Jorge — that's the nurse — pulled the IV tube out of her arm and said she was done for the day.

"What?" I couldn't believe it. "Not come any more?" I'd been stretched out in the empty chair beside hers. I kicked down the footrest and it rocketed me up straight, so it looked like I was really mad, which I was. "Why?"

"I don't want you here, little darling." She was digging around in her makeup bag for something. "This place is full of sick people. It's depressing."

"No, it's not! Justin and Kwan said they'd teach us cribbage. Chibundu's bringing the snacks tomorrow and —"

"I just don't think it's the right place for you." She slathered on some lipstick and smacked off the extra.

"So what? I like it here. And what else would I be doing? It's not like I —"

"Oh, look at the time." She didn't even pretend to check her watch. She just scrunched her hair and picked up her bags and started leaving.

"Gidge!"

She waved to the others. "Toodle-oo, amigos! Hasta la vista!"

"Gidge!" I scrambled up and ran after her.

I kept my voice down until we got to the street, then I argued with her all the way to Over Easy. I was still going, "Pleeeeeeease, Gidge," when we stepped into the shop.

Con stopped dusting and went, "Pleeeeeeease what?"

Gidge immediately gave him her side of the story. Before I even had a chance to give him mine, he said, "Why doesn't Yardley just hang out at the shop while you get your chemo? I'm sure Harris would love the company!" I didn't have a chance after that.

Gidge said, "What a wonderful idea! You'll love it here, YaYa, and I won't have to worry about you." She lowered herself into the Barcalounger with a big happy sigh and started touching up her eyeliner. Con suddenly had to re-arrange the sandal display. Neither of them would look at me. That's when I knew exactly what was up. They were match-making. They were going to force a friend on me whether I liked it or not.

I knew Harris wasn't crazy about the idea either, because as soon as Con went into his office Harris did too. I could hear him whisper-screaming that he didn't want me there, that he was happier before I showed up. Con closed the door. Everything was too quiet for a while, then Harris schlepped out and looked at me as if I'd ruined his life.

Every morning after that, I'd arrive at the shop and it would be the same thing: Harris, hating me with his face. I just had to do that *la-la-la* thing in my head. How else could I block him out? If karma hadn't been watching, I would have sneered back. See how he liked it. Instead, I'd just smile and ask Con what I could do to help. If I was lucky, he'd have a mannequin that needed restyling. (I definitely preferred plastic people to some of the real ones.)

One night when I was back home from Over Easy and Gidge was back from the hospital, she asked me how things were going with Harris.

"They're not," I said. "Which is just the way I like it, thank you very much."

"YaYa . . ."

"What?" We were snuggled on her bed watching *Queer Eye*.

"Don't say that. It's not nice."

"I'm not allowed to tell the truth now?"

"You should be more open to Harris. He's a smart kid. You two have a lot in common."

"Like what? We're both horrible?"

"You're only horrible when you're trying to get a rise out of me. And Harris . . ." She searched for the word. "He's just a little prickly — but that's normal. You should have seen your father at that age." She went, "Woo!" and laughed. "That's when he started calling himself Fred. Did you know that?"

If she thought she was going to distract me, she was sadly mistaken. I knew this story. Dad's real name was Freedom, but he changed it in junior high when adult diapers called "Freedom for Men" came out. He thought Gidge would be upset, but she just said, "Fred. Hmm. Suits you. Wish I'd thought of that myself."

Gidge was getting geared up to tell it to me again but I went, "Yeah, well, Harris isn't my father," by which I meant my KooKoo, "and I don't like him."

"Don't like him *now*," Gidge said, as if I just needed a little practice or something. She took a tiny bite of a biscuit. The chemo made her sick to her stomach so she always had to have something tasteless to nibble on.

"Ever." I sat up straight and folded my arms. (It's hard to look mad when you're snuggling.)

"You never know what another person is dealing with, darling. Things aren't going very well for Harris at the moment, but he holds it in. I knew someone like that once, someone who hid their feelings too. I didn't realize they were sad — every bit as sad as I was — and so I wasn't very nice to them. I'm ashamed of myself now."

"I don't believe you." Gidge would never have been mean to anyone. "You're just trying to make me like Harris. You're just making up another life lesson."

"I wish I were. I really hurt this person. But not half as

much as I hurt myself, of course. That's what happens with these things." She tipped her chin down and smiled at me. Her eyes were big and the green part was all speckled and swirly. She should have been a hypnotist. "So I'd love you to make an effort with Harris. And not just for my sake. Or for his. For your sake, too."

Gidge went back to watching *Queer Eye* but I sat there and got really mad. Trying to pawn some random friend off on me as if I was so desperate any old one would do! Why did I have to be nice to Harris when I didn't like him and he didn't like me?

Because Gidge was dying?

Yes.

Because being good was the only way I was going to be able to keep her?

Yes.

Because I needed the karma points?

Yes.

"Okay," I said, and almost smiled. "He's not that bad." And he wasn't. Harris was probably more or less okay for a human being, just not *my* human being. "But I'd rather be in the hospital with you. Can't I come? Please. I'll be good. I'll be quiet. It's not depressing at all! *Please.*"

I went on like that for a while. I was getting kind of annoyed — I hated it when she didn't answer me — then I realized her eyes were closed and her breathing had slowed down. She did that a lot — just up and fell asleep on me. "That's what happens with cancer," she'd said when I got mad at her once about it. Now I was just mad at the cancer.

I took the teacup out of her hand and put it on the bedside table. She'd been reading the paper earlier and it was folded in half on the table too. I picked it up. She'd circled an article about a lady they called "The Free-Gift Queen" because of all the prizes she'd won in online contests. I don't remember if I thought it was weird or not — Gidge usually didn't care about stuff like that — but I noticed the article and I remembered it later. (You should remember it too. But if you forget, don't worry. I'll remind you.) I put the paper back on the table then I curled up on the bed beside Gidge. If she wanted me to hang out with stupid Harris, fine. I'd hang out with stupid Harris.

I'd have done anything for Gidge. That's how much she meant to me.

Means to me.

As in *now*.

CHAPTER 10

Remember I said Gidge had to do three things? One was to call a family meeting. Two was to get her karma in order. Now we're at the Number Three Thing Gidge had to do: die.

She could have just held on until it happened naturally, but "Why wait?" she said at our worst family meeting ever. "As the famous singer Bob Dylan once put it, 'Be groovy or leave, man.' And I ain't groovy anymore."

No one laughed.

She told us she'd been talking to a doctor about it for a while. Everything was all organized. She'd made an appointment to die the following Friday.

It wasn't fair. It was only six weeks since she'd told us she had cancer and already she was saying "Why wait?" Wasn't the reason obvious?

So you don't break my heart and make me sad forever.

But when I tried to tell her that, my throat closed up and my eyes started stinging and I ended up just stomping out of the kitchen like I didn't care. I sat on my bed and started bedazzling my skort again. The day I heard she had cancer, I threw the stupid thing across my room and promised I'd never touch it ever again. But why shouldn't I? If Gidge wanted to die so bad, then I could do whatever I damn well pleased (including not putting twenty-five cents in the swear jar for saying "damn").

There was a knock at my door.

"Go away," I said.

Mima and Pa came in.

"I said go away."

They crawled onto my skinny little bed and sat on either side of me. They were so close I could barely move. It was like the bus at rush hour, only all the other seats were empty.

"I want to finish this," I said.

"Gidge is tired," Pa said.

"So what? I don't need her. You think I don't know how to bedazzle or something?"

"She's in pain. Her body's had enough. None of us wants her to go."

"*She* doesn't want to go!" Mima added. "She'd stay if she could. You know she would."

"But it's time. She's done everything she can for us except

live forever. It's not fair to make her suffer any longer." Pa rubbed his beard against my head. "If the doctor helps her die, Gidge'll get to go the way she wants to go. And you know how she likes doing things her own way." He tried to chuckle, but even he's not that good an actor.

I didn't answer. I just sat there not doing anything — not bedazzling, not breathing, not even crying. Mima and Pa were quiet too, except for their hearts, which were pounding against my arms like I was a punching bag or something.

Then Pa got his happy voice back and said, "Gidge really hopes you'll help her plan her big day. She wants a fabulous celebration of this life before she starts her next one. So she needs you. She needs 'YaYa's magic touch.' Those were her *exact* words."

Good one, Pa. Telling me that. Now what was I going to do? Be the evil grand-fairy and not grant my favorite person her dying wish? I could hardly go and ruin her death — *especially* since she'd been so excited about it and everything.

I squeezed the bedazzler as hard as I could and nailed an amber sparkle onto the pocket of my skort. Not exactly where I wanted it to go, but whatever. It wasn't the worst thing that had happened to me that day.

"Okay. Fine," I said. "I'll help her."

"You're a good kid," Mima said.

"But I'm not going to like it." It was important they knew that.

"You don't have to like it," Pa said.

"Yeah, well, I'm actually going to *hate* it."

"When you love someone, sometimes you have to do things you hate for them."

I was going to say, *So why doesn't Gidge just keep living, then? She loves us, doesn't she?* But I didn't. By then, I kind of knew the answer, so I said fine, I'd help her. Pa and Mima hugged me really hard, then left. I was glad they did. That type of hugging always makes me cry, and there was no way I was going to let them see me cry.

CHAPTER 11

Usually when you plan for a "big day" it's Halloween or your birthday or the summer solstice and you can hardly wait until it happens. *It's going to be really fun! Everyone's going to be so happy! It's going to be a huge celebration!*

Not Gidge's big day. I was spending all my time planning for the worst possible thing ever. Gidge and I would be in her room choosing the clothes she was going to wear, or the food we were going to eat, or exactly how mixy-matchy she wanted the bedsheets to be, and I'd be feeling really happy because this was totally the type of stuff Gidge and I loved to do, and then — *splat!* — I'd suddenly remember why I was doing it, and it was like my heart got stomped on by a professional wrestler. Gidge believed in reincarnation, and I *wanted* to — like, really, really wanted to — but it was hard. I was terrified she'd die and I'd lose her forever. That's the scariest feeling in the world. It's like being tied to the tracks with a train coming at you. You don't even need it to happen to know how much it's going to hurt.

I'd turn away and pinch myself super hard so at least I'd have something else to cry about. Then Gidge would make some joke or ask me to go into the kitchen to see if there was any more of that tea she liked, and I'd leave and have to stay away until my face unsplotched and I could breathe again without making squeaking sounds.

Because that was the other thing Gidge told us at that family meeting: no more tears. She wanted us to keep dancing until she left the party. That's what she said.

I tried my best. My throat hurt from holding everything in and my arms were covered with purple pinch marks.

"Somebody abusing you or what?" Harris said when I wore a sleeveless mini dress to Over Easy one day.

Con went, "Harris!"

He wanted to send him to the stockroom for the rest of the day, but I said, "It's all right. I don't mind." I needed to be nice because I knew it was good for my karma, but I couldn't do it for very long. It made my face hurt and my stomach go all jittery. I waited until it didn't look like it was Harris's fault, then I told Con I was going to go home earlier. Con said, "Good idea." He knew I didn't have much time left to spend with Gidge.

The nurse had started coming to the house every morning but she was gone by the time I got there. Gidge didn't get out of bed much anymore. She still talked and smiled and laughed, only she did it slower and, like, *smaller* now. That day, the painkillers had made her too sleepy to even do that, so I got out an old scarf I'd been making and just sat next to her on the bed knitting. I tried to tell myself that was enough. I could still see her and smell her and touch her. Gidge always said you shouldn't be greedy but I didn't care. I was greedy for Gidge. I stopped going to Over Easy after that.

The next Friday came way too fast. "Black Friday" I called it, but not the kind where you go shopping. Black as in sad. Black as in all the lights have gone out and you don't know where the switch is.

I woke up early that day. I was sleeping on a cot in Gidge's room, so close we could hold hands if we needed to. Her eyes were shut but I could tell she was awake. Her mouth was smiling. "Hear the birds, little darling?" It sounded like she was whispering, but that was just the way she talked now. "Lovely, aren't they?"

No, I thought.

I crawled onto her bed, careful not to jiggle things too much because, by then, even a jiggle could hurt her. I curled up against her side and rubbed her nails with the tip of my finger, the way I used to when I was little. I'd painted them "Scarlet Inferno" for her the night before. The red looked savage next to the purple stone in her ring.

A few minutes later my parents came in. Mima was carrying a tray with warm croissants and fresh strawberries and the poo vase full of Gidge's favorite flowers. Pa had a bottle of champagne in one hand and four upside-down wine glasses hanging off the fingers of his other. (I'll always hate champagne. It's the saddest drink in the world.)

Pa had trimmed his beard and slicked back his hair and was wearing a shiny black tuxedo he'd worn in a play. Mima was wearing a party dress from the same play and burgundy lipstick. She'd stuck two little curls onto her cheeks with spit. It was weird seeing my parents like that when they weren't on stage. They never got dressed up if they didn't have to. This was an excellent example of people doing something they hated for someone they loved.

"Morning, Gidge," Pa said. "Welcome to the first day of the rest of your life."

She laughed. "Welcome indeed, my darling. And what a way to kick it off!" She was struggling to sit up, so Mima and Pa put all their stuff down really fast and helped her.

They sent me upstairs to put on my best clothes: a cyber-boho wench's costume from their Robin-Hood-in-Space play. When I got back, Mima and Pa had Gidge all made-up and dressed. She was wearing a silk kimono with a dragon on the back, gigantic purple drop earrings and this turban sort of thing I'd made just a few days before from some old scarves because the chemo had made all her hair fall out and all she had left was white fuzz that reminded me of cat hair and almost made me sneeze just looking at it. I want to say she looked beautiful, but she didn't. She was so tiny now and her head was so big and her eyes so buggy she kind of looked like Dobby the house-elf. I had to just keep reminding myself that wasn't Gidge's real face.

Mima arranged the croissants and strawberries on the bedside table. Pa popped open the champagne and poured us all a glass, even though it's illegal for twelve-year-olds to drink and I didn't want it anyway. Then Mima banged a gong and they did this little skit they'd written called "A Smidgen of Gidge." They acted out her entire life in seven and a half minutes — including Pa pretending to be Gidge giving birth to Pa, very weird — and we laughed so hard it looked like that's where the tears were coming from. Then Gidge said, "What time is it?" and Mima said, "Eight-thirty," and Gidge said, "Oh, dear, better get a move on, then. Dr. Wallace is coming at nine!" And that kind of killed the mood, and we were quiet for a while, until Gidge said, "Izzy?"

Mima said, "Yes?" because Izzy's her real name. Mima is just something I called her when I was little.

"You're my very favorite daughter-in-law, darling, so you get to be first."

Mima went and sat next to the bed. They held hands and whispered to each other and they kissed and whispered some more and kissed and kissed, then Gidge patted Mima's hand and then Mima sucked in her breath really loud and got up and came over and sat next to me.

Then Gidge said, "Fred . . . Freedom . . . Can I call you that just this one time? A silly name, I know, but today, it seems so fitting," and Pa said, "Of course, of course," like he would have let her call him anything she wanted. Then he sat next to her and they did the same thing as Mima and Gidge did, kissing and hugging and whispering, even though Pa was crying so hard I'm pretty sure Gidge couldn't understand a word he said. She pushed his face back and rubbed his tears from his cheeks and down into his beard, and they looked at each other for a long, long time, then she said, "Sorry, but I have to go, darling. I need to speak to YaYa before the doctor comes," and he nodded and got up and wiped his sleeve across his face and wouldn't look at me.

And then it was my turn. Mima gave me a little shove and I walked over to the bed, my legs all wiggly, and I took Gidge's hand, and I opened my mouth, but I couldn't say anything. Not a thing. Not even "I love you," which I'd said to Gidge a thousand times a day for as long as I could remember.

She looked me straight in the eyes and I forgot Dobby the house-elf and I saw her real face again, and she said, "That's okay. We don't need to say anything." Her voice was tiny and slow and scratchy. "Our hearts know."

That wasn't enough and never would be. "Don't go, Gidge," I said.

"I have to, little darling. Don't worry. It's just my silly old body. You get to keep the rest of me forever. Just look for me. That's all you have to do. I'll never leave you. You know that."

"Never?" I said.

"Never, ever, ever." She shook her head and then she smiled. "You be good now. Good and brave and loving and kind."

"I will." My voice had gone croaky from holding everything in. "I'm going to be all those things. I promise, Gidge. I promise." I looked hard into her eyes and right down into her insides so she'd know I was telling the truth. My karma was going to be so perfect the universe would have to give her back to me.

She touched my cheek with her fingers. They were very cold. "And will you do one more thing for me?"

"Anything."

"Will you make sure your father puts down the toilet seat?"

We both laughed at that because we knew Pa wouldn't remember unless I bugged him, and just when I was sort of feeling a tiny bit normal again, there was a knock at the bedroom door and the doctor stuck his head in.

"Good morning, Gidge," he said. "It's nine o'clock. Are you ready for me?" He didn't look like a doctor and he didn't look sad. His hair was gray and curly and a bit too long, like he was a maestro or something. He was wearing a black turtleneck and glasses with big yellow frames. I had this funny feeling that maybe he'd been one of her students too, but nobody said anything about that so maybe he wasn't. I could tell he was the type of person she'd like, though.

"Yes, come in, come in, Dr. Wallace!" Gidge said. "Can we tempt you with a little champagne?"

"I'd love some," he said, "but I'd better not." Then he asked her if she was sure about her decision, if she understood what was happening, and if she could confirm that no one was forcing her into it. And she said, yes, yes, yes, smiling the whole time.

Then he said, "Okay. We can get started. I'm going to give you a drug first to make you sleepy, and once you lose consciousness, I'm going to give you another drug that will stop your heart."

"Nothing will stop my heart," she said.

And he looked at her like that was the wrong answer, like maybe she *didn't* really understand after all, but she croaked out a little laugh and said, "Metaphorically speaking! My physical heart will stop beating but my spirit will go on."

"Ah . . ." He smiled. "Well, I'm sure if anyone's spirit is

going to live on, it's yours, Gidge — but the drug I'm about to give you *will* make your body die. Make no mistake about it." He looked straight at her, all serious again. "Understood?"

"Aye, aye, Captain. Understood."

"Are you ready, then? Shall I proceed?"

No. Say no, Gidge! That's what was screaming inside my head but she said, "Yes," right away. "I'm ready, Dr. Wallace. Fred just has to turn on the music for me. Can't make my grand exit without my soundtrack."

Pa cranked up the music and the doctor gave Gidge a needle. Pa held her hand, Mima rubbed her feet and I snuggled up beside her. She kissed me and whispered, "Stay wild, Moon Child," which was kind of a joke because she used to say that to me when I was little and having a tantrum, then she fell asleep to her favorite song. It's by a band called Blood, Sweat & Tears and it's called "You've Made Me So Very Happy" and it's exactly what I felt about her but now she was going and I'd never feel that way again.

Dr. Wallace gave her another drug, but nothing happened, just her breathing got really slow and kind of dizzy-making and our hearts started thumping really loud.

After a while — I don't know how long — Gidge made this weird rattly noise, and we all looked up kind of happy because we thought she was clearing her throat to say something to us, but the doctor just smiled sadly and shook his head. A few minutes later, he took her wrist in his hand, then he listened to her heart with his stethoscope, then he nodded.

"She's gone." Then, just to rub it in or something, he said, "She's dead." He wouldn't let us hope even a little bit.

We all started crying pretty loud, so at first I didn't notice the song had changed, but then I heard Richie Havens singing, "Here comes the sun." I don't know if you know the song but that's pretty much the whole thing. He's singing to his little darling and he just says the same words, over and over again, until he goes, "It's all right."

I looked out the window, expecting to see blue sky, but it was raining, as in *pouring*, as if the sky was sobbing too or something. Richie just kept growling away about the sun coming and it being all right.

No, I thought. *It's all wrong. Everything he said is wrong.*

Then I thought: *It's not about the real sun. It's the metaphorical sun. The sun in my head.*

I realized it was a message from Gidge. I'm Gidge's little darling and she was telling me she was okay, and it was going to be all right. I didn't actually smile or anything, but I was glad to hear from her.

CHAPTER 12

Spoiler alert: It took a long time, but things did turn out all right in the end.

That's because there was a Number Four Thing Gidge did too. I didn't find out about it until way later.

I'll tell you what it was, but I've got to tell you everything else that happened first. It's the only way this'll make sense.

I also don't want to ruin the surprise because that would really bug Gidge. She loved surprises. Almost as much as she loved mysteries of the universe. And this is kind of both.

CHAPTER 13

Gidge was gone, but she was still kind of there, too. It was like in cartoons when someone takes off really fast and there's a little cloud left where the person used to be. Gidge's cloud smelled like lavender and green tea and the ointment she used on her knees and something else that's hard to describe but I like a lot. I was scared if I left the house even for a second I'd come back and the cloud would have disappeared, and then what would I do? That's the only reason I didn't run off and fling myself immediately into The Pit of Despair. I didn't want to lose her.

Mima and Pa tiptoed around the house with brave looks on their faces, as if that was going to make everything okay. They kept asking me how I was feeling but I didn't want to talk about it. They tried to get me to go to a grief counselor with them but I didn't want to do that either. They finally just gave up. I went into Gidge's room and pulled down the blinds.

They left me meals by the door but I didn't eat. I didn't change my clothes. I barely peed. I tried not to think because all I had left to think about were bad things. I kept wishing I was a mannequin. They get to wear nice clothes and don't have to think about anything.

But then this one morning, about a week later, I woke up dreaming Gidge was alive and I felt okay. Somehow, I knew that as long as I didn't look at the empty spot in the room where she was supposed to be I'd feel good the whole day. I'd kept a hunk of her hair from when the chemo made it fall out. I hot-glued it onto a barrette and decided to wear it all the time. I felt like I had a little piece of Gidge growing out of my brain. I got out my embroidery project — a rainbow-colored flying squirrel on the back of an old jean jacket — and went to work. I kept my eye on my sewing and just talked to Dead Gidge the way I'd always talked to Live Gidge. Dead Gidge didn't answer, at least not out loud, but I pretty much knew what she would have said so I just filled in the blanks. I brought her tea when I made my breakfast and always asked if she needed anything whenever I had to leave the room. I wasn't hallucinating. It's not like I'd lost touch with reality or anything. I just decided I didn't want to spend quite so much time with it. Gidge always said, "Imagine the world the way you want it to be and anything is possible." That's all I was doing, imagining my perfect world.

It worked pretty well until Mima stuck her head in the door one day. "Who are you talking to in there?"

"Ah . . . nobody," I said, but she looked so freaked out I knew I was going to have to keep our conversations private. From then on, Dead Gidge and I only talked in my head.

I would have been happy to stay in her room forever, just the two of us, but a few days later Con called, all in a panic. "I got twelve bags of the most gorgeous formal wear from an estate sale and it has to be steamed and priced and hung. Any chance you'd come in and give me a hand?"

The answer was no, and I almost said so, but then Dead Gidge whispered in my ear, "YaYa . . . karma! Don't forget about your karma."

She was right. The universe wasn't going to give her back to me if I didn't help Con when he needed me. My heart hurt but I got dressed — cropped plaid pants, polka-dot shirt, statement belt and my Gidge barrette — and dragged myself back to Over Easy.

It wasn't so bad. Con looked almost as sad as I did, which was nice. He didn't do irritating things like try to distract me or make me laugh. He talked about Gidge when I wanted to and never said "She's in a better place," as if I should be happy she died or something.

I started going to Over Easy every day. It gave me lots of stuff to tell Dead Gidge about when I got back home, plus it made Pa and Mima happy. They were working hard at the theater again and didn't like me being alone all day. Even better, Con always let me do the window displays now. Weird thing was, after a while, I realized I liked dealing with the customers too, even though they were strangers. Someone would come out of the dressing room in a new outfit and I'd be, like, *brain wave!* I'd suddenly know just the slingback wedges or puka-shell choker to really make the look pop. "Let me Gidge you up," I'd say.

The only reason I *didn't* like going to Over Easy was that Harris was still there. My first day back, he shuffled over to me and said, "Sorry about your grandmother," but he was looking at the floor when he said it, and I could tell by the way Con was pretending not to watch that he'd forced him into it, so I didn't really believe Harris was sorry about anything, except maybe getting stuck in the shop with me again.

I said, "Thank you," which I didn't mean either, and he schlepped back to the Barcalounger. Now that Gidge was gone, he had it all to himself. He'd sit there all hunched up over his book until Con would say "It's time you got a little exercise" and hand him the Swiffer or the window squeegee or some boxes that needed to be squished flat. Other than that, Harris would *occasionally* take a moment out of his busy day to sneer at me, but mostly he just did his best to pretend I didn't exist.

The worst part of the day was when Con took his break at three-thirty. He'd leave the two of us alone in the store for a quick power-walk then trot back exactly half an hour later with the mail and some snacks for us.

I had lots of stuff to do in the shop while he was gone, so it wasn't as if Harris and I spent much time *interacting*, but still. The vibes he gave off. If someone came in and commented on my window display or the mannequin I'd dressed he'd do this thing that I can only describe as *rolling his eyes out loud*. I didn't get why he was so mad all the time. Gidge used to say that if you hold on to anger, it'll just keep building and building until one day it'll explode. I couldn't help picturing my beautiful window display all splattered with little bits of Harris and no one around to clean it up but me.

One day, just a little while after I started going back to Over Easy, Con came in from his walk and went, "Yardley! I've got something for you!"

"Croissants?" I said. They were my favorite.

"Something even better." He waved an envelope at me.

It looked like it was made out of squished wet Kleenex and, even from where I was standing by the counter, I could see it had a big red kiss on the back.

CHAPTER 14

I grabbed the letter from Con and held it against my face.
I didn't know if there was a kiss still left in the lipstick, but
I did get a tiny whiff of Gidge's cloud. I ran my finger over the
corner of the envelope where she'd typed her name and address.

```
The Being formerly known as Gidge O'Hanlon,
          Riding a Shooting Star
     Somewhere in The Vast Unknown.
```

I laughed. I put the card against my chest and glanced
around the shop. I had this weird feeling that she was there
with me, that this whole stupid death thing had all been a bad
joke and any second now she was going to pop out of the
dressing room or walk through the door or — I don't know
— poof out of the envelope in a swirl of sparkles like a fairy
princess in a Disney movie. My heart was going nuts.

I tore the envelope open and started reading.

Greetings, Earthling!
I'm writing this in Con's office
several weeks before it will come
sailing into your world from the
other side.
As I prepare for my next big
journey, I'm so grateful for the
special times the cosmos allowed me
to spend with you. I'm filled with joy
thinking of all the love and laughter
we shared bringing beauty to our
little corner of Creation. Believe it
or not, I'm even happy thinking about
the not-so-good stuff too --- like
when money was short, or kindness
hard to come by, or even when those
nasty old cancer cells decided to
take over my earthly self. How lucky
we are to have found kindred spirits
to weather the storms with!
I know things are hard for you
now, YaYa, but that's okay. Good,
bad, happy, sad, exciting, boring,

terrific or terrifying --- all
experience is part of the wondrous
adventure called life.

Don't hide from it, Little
Darling. Enjoy it all, the beauty and
the bumps. Make the most of each
glorious moment. It won't be long
before you find someone new to take my
place. Welcome them with open arms.
Let them see how wonderful you are.
I'll be with you every hop, skip and
bump along the way.

See you soon!

Your ever-loving Gidge

XOXOXOXOXO times a gazillion

CHAPTER 15

C on went, "Are you laughing or crying?"

I had to think about it. I wiggled the card back into the envelope. "Both," I said, and I tried not to be embarrassed. "It's from Gidge."

"I know. She asked me to mail it for her. How is she?" He twinkled a bit when he said that.

"The same. She wrote, 'Greetings, Earthlings!' instead of 'Dear Yardley.' And she told me she'd be seeing me soon but it doesn't feel like it. It feels like she's gone forever, and I know I'm not supposed to think that but I do. It's like knives in my head it hurts so bad. Even worse. Swords or something." I wiped the inside of my elbow over my face. "Gidge said it's okay to feel that way. It's all part of life so I'm supposed to like it, but I don't."

I'm not sure Con could understand me because I had trouble getting the words out. Sometimes I said them when I was sucking in a big breath and other times I said them when I was burping one out. A customer came into the store but Con went, "Out! Out!" and flicked his hand at her.

He looked at me with his head tipped to the side and his bottom lip curled down like a flower petal. He said, "But do you know what's okay too? A hug from friends when you're feeling sad." He walked over to me with his arms out. "Right, Harris?"

He turned and looked. Harris had disappeared into the office again.

Con hugged me. "Ah, honey. I'm sorry. You don't need him acting like that now, do you?"

I shrugged. "I don't mind."

And I really and truly didn't. A hug from someone who didn't like me would have been way worse than no hug at all.

CHAPTER 16

Over the next couple of days, other letters came. Mima and Pa each got one. I don't know exactly what the letters said, but right after they read them, Pa announced they were going to do *Macbeth* next season and we had chocolate fudge cake for dinner that day and danced until midnight.

Con got one too. He arrived back from the post office, hung his fedora on the hat hook and disappeared into his office. When he came out twenty minutes later, his face was splotchy but his smile was huge.

I looked up from the gaucho pants I was hemming. "What did she say?" It wasn't any of my business but sometimes I just can't control myself.

Con thought about it for a second, then said, "Everything I needed to hear." He got on the phone and asked if the storefront next door was for rent too. He wanted to add a menswear section to the shop.

A day later, Con bounded in the door, waving an envelope and hollering, "Special delivery for Mr. Harris K. Park!" Harris didn't smile or say thanks or jump up and down like the rest of us had. He just shoved it into his pocket as if it was some old chocolate bar wrapper and went back to his stupid puzzle book.

I was so mad. Harris didn't deserve a letter if he was going to treat it like that. A letter from Gidge should be treated like a treasure. I'd wrapped mine in tissue paper so the kiss on the back wouldn't smudge and tucked it away in the counter drawer to keep it safe. I took it out and read it whenever I needed a little pick-me-up.

Make the most of each glorious moment, Gidge had written to me, so I tried. I focused on doing things I liked. The more good stuff I crammed into me, the less room there was for the bad stuff. That's what I figured.

I liked decorating the shop window, so I did that. I liked going through the bags of clothes people brought in to sell. I liked finding customers the exact right thing to wear. When they bought it, which they usually did — I know that sounds conceited but it's true — I liked folding it perfectly, then wrapping it in three sheets of aqua-blue tissue paper, closing it with an Over Easy sticker, and then carefully, carefully, carefully slipping it into a shopping bag without scrunching anything.

When I really, really needed to fill myself with good stuff though, I'd go through the racks until I found something that used to be Gidge's. I'd pull it out, hold it really close to my face and pretend I was checking for moth holes so Harris wouldn't know what I was up to. The clothes had all been cleaned but every so often I could still catch a hint of Gidge's cloud. That usually helped.

Most of her clothes had gotten snapped up pretty fast but there were still a few good things hanging around. I particularly loved a pair of super-high-waisted matador pants done in a steel-blue metallic plaid — but my very, very favorite thing wasn't on the floor yet. It was this long green velvet dress with a halter neckline and little puckers at the bodice where your boobs would go if you had any. I'd been awestruck the first time I'd seen it, but Gidge had taken one peek at it and gone, "Ack!" as if she'd swallowed a bug. "I can't even look at that dress."

This was back when we were cleaning out The Wardrobe Department, before we'd even *heard* of Over Easy. She was sitting on her bed, drinking lukewarm ginger tea. Her hair was spread out over the cushions I'd piled up behind her. She looked like a retired mermaid.

I was like, "What? Can't look at it?! Why? This is perfect!"

"No," she said. "No, it's not." She closed her eyes and started breathing hard through her nostrils the way she did when she saw someone be rude to a waitress. For a second there I thought I'd made her mad, but then she opened her eyes and smiled.

"It's just a plain old maxi dress."

"Plain," I went, as in, *C'mon!*

"Yup. Plain. In the sixties, they were *de rigueur*," she said, meaning "normal" but kind of making fun of herself for saying it that way. "We'd wear them with sandals and long beads and enormous floppy hats. They were practically the hippie uniform."

"It's *gorge-wah!*" I said, which was a pretend French word we used for a while there. "I bet you looked amazing in it. You must have worn it all the time."

"No." She gave her head a little shake and took a sip of tea. "Only wore it once."

I held it up in front of her and tipped my head one way, then the other. The green was totally her color. With her eyes and her pale skin and how black her hair used to be — I mean, *wow*. "How come?"

"I don't know . . ." She stared into her cup a long time before answering. "It just didn't bring out the best in me, I guess." This was a humongous understatement, but it would be a while before I found that out, and even longer before I believed it.

I asked if I could keep the dress, but Gidge went, "Oh, darling . . . ," like that was such a silly idea. "It's too big for you." Even after I'd explained how there's a little something known as "growth spurts" she still wouldn't give it to me. She wouldn't even talk about it anymore.

I didn't see the dress again until a few days after we'd all got our letters. Con had left for his afternoon walk to the post office. Harris was stretched out on the Barcalounger, doing I didn't know what exactly, probably just trying to come up with a twelve-letter word meaning "Yardley bugs me" or something. I was sitting on a stool behind the counter, going through a big freezer bag full of costume jewelry someone had dropped off. I'd just discovered a pair of chunky black-and-white Bakelite button earrings and realized they'd look absolutely fab with my weeding outfit. That made me all shivery *ooh-ooh-ooh*-happy for a second there, but it didn't last long. Out of nowhere, Dead Gidge dive-bombed me.

That's what Pa calls it when everything's going okay and suddenly you get this little movie in your head of Gidge talking or laughing or doing something totally normal like yawning or sneezing and, just like that — *splurch* — the truth hits you smack in the face: Gidge is dead.

The tip of my nose began to prickle and my eyes started to sting and I knew what was coming. I was going to cry again, right there in the shop. I thought, *Oh, great*, and pinched myself. Even if I tried my hardest, I wouldn't enjoy crying with Harris watching.

I was pinching myself and biting my lip and squeezing my legs together as if I needed to pee, doing anything I could think of to keep myself from losing it, when the bell over the door tinkled and a lady walked in. I pulled myself together and said hello.

Con always says, "Our clothes are older than our customers," but that wasn't true this time. The lady was at least Gidge's age. Her hair was straight and silver and cut in a perfect bob. She was wearing a pale pink linen suit. It looked great on her, which sounds funny to say because Gidge and I were never crazy about pastels. The lady's oversized glasses were a bold choice and a nice contrast to her hair and outfit.

I put the earrings down and said, "Welcome to Over Easy," just the way Con told us to say it.

She smiled and went, "Lovely shop." She rubbed the hem of a burnt-orange silk blouse I'd put on one of the mannequins and did this *oooh* thing with her lips.

"Can I help you find something?" I was already thinking of outfits she'd look good in.

"Not today, I'm afraid. I'm in a bit of a rush. Just popping by to pick up a package." She had a raspy voice, the kind singers have, the ones who can really belt it out. Gidge's voice was a bit like that too. "The name's Johnson."

"A package?" Con hadn't mentioned anything to me about it, but I figured he'd probably forgotten. He'd been really busy with the new fall clothes starting to come in. "Do you know what it is?"

The lady laughed. "No. Just that it's a free gift of some sort."

You'd think I'd have remembered Gidge circling that article in the paper about The Free Gift Queen, but I didn't. Never even crossed my mind. I went, "Hmm . . ." and took a quick look under the counter, on the shelves, in the cupboard where Con keeps the extra bags. "Nothing here. You're sure you're in the right shop? Over Easy?"

"Good question! I'd better check. I've always been a bit of a contest junkie. I fill out so many prize forms, I lose track!" She took a letter out of her purse and read it. "Yup. 'Congratulations! You've won the Let Bygones Be Bygones prize at Over Easy.' That's what it says."

"It's probably in the office, then. Harris, would you mind?" I smiled at him because it's important to appear professional. Harris gave a big sigh but got up to look.

"Thank you. Very kind," the lady said and put the letter back in her purse. "In the meantime, I'll just sneak a peek at some of the gorgeous things you have here." She hummed along to the music on the speakers as she went through the racks, looking at each piece of clothing, checking out the cut, the fabric, even the seams, same as Gidge and I always did.

There was something about her I liked. I didn't know what it was, but I felt it right away and that is *so not me*.

I don't like new things, especially when they're people.

"Oh, would you look at this!" She took out a mustard-yellow jacket with giant padded shoulders and skinny lapels. "Isn't it fabulous? So eighties! I had no idea this shop was even here. Had I known! Like a walk down memory lane."

I smiled and went back to my bag of jewelry. Other than the Bakelite earrings, most of the stuff was pretty *whatever* — bent bangles, rings with missing rhinestones, chokers that didn't quite close — but then . . . *jackpot*. I pulled out this insane necklace. Laughing monkeys about the size of animal cookies, held together by their tails. Tacky but, like, *good* tacky. My brain started bubbling with possible wardrobe combos.

I was just considering a fitted black turtleneck over a barkcloth skirt when I heard Harris schlep back in.

"Is your name Mrs. Margaret Johnson?" He held a big brown shipping envelope up to his face and read, "Address: 1131 —"

The lady went, "Yes, that's me!" and wiggled her fingers until he gave her the envelope. "How exciting! I wonder what's in it. Mind if I open it here?"

"Sure," I said. Gidge and I were like that too. We could never wait.

She put the envelope on the top of the rack next to her, stuck her pointer finger in the little gap where the flap was taped down, then wiggled it back and forth until it tore open.

She peeked inside and smiley-frowned, the way you do on your birthday when you've got half the wrapping off but you can't figure out what the present is yet.

"Hmmm . . . ," she said, reaching her hand in. "Ooh, this is going to be good! It feels lovely."

She lifted her eyebrows way up in excitement — then pulled out Gidge's green velvet dress.

The lady made a choking sound and slapped her hand over her mouth. At first, I thought it was because she liked it so much, but then I took another look. Her eyes had gone huge, and kind of blinky, too, as if she was having trouble focusing. She went, "My, my, my, my . . . dress! My dress!" I wasn't getting happy vibes.

"*Your* dress?" I said. "What do you mean — *yours?*"

She didn't answer. She dragged her hand through her hair and stared at the dress.

She inspected the zipper, the ruffles, the hem. She even held it up and smelled it. She turned to Harris and went, "Where did you get this?" as if he'd stolen it or something. "Where did you get my dress?"

"The . . . uh . . . office?" He pointed over his shoulder then looked at me, like, *What's going on?*

I came out from behind the counter. "I'm sorry but you must be mistaken." I tried to maintain a polite manner. That's what Con told us to do if we ever had to deal with a "problem client" while he was out. "This is a vintage garment that belonged to —"

"I am *not* mistaken." She was holding the dress up tight to her chin, as if she was bare naked and that's all she had covering her. "It's my dress. Mine."

She shoved it back into the envelope.

"Ah . . . no. Sorry. Maybe you had a dress that *looked* like it, but this was my grandmother's. She made it."

"Your *grandmother?*" The lady went really white. She waved one hand in front of her face. She didn't look so good.

It suddenly dawned on me what might be happening. Gidge had a friend who used to get confused too. Dehydration can be hard on old people.

"Why don't you have a seat and let me get you something to drink?" I took a step toward her, but something about her face made me stop dead in my tracks. She'd been looking at me before but now she was, like, *looking at me.* Looking at me as if she knew me.

That's when I realized what was actually happening. You know that tick-tock sound they play on game shows when the host is pointing his index card at the board and everybody's waiting to find out if the contestant's right and the tension's building, building, building until suddenly there's this *whoosh!* and the answer flashes on the screen and the audience goes crazy and confetti starts falling down from the ceiling? That's what this was like. I heard the *tick-tick-tick-whoosh* in my head and then the answer just came to me. I was so shocked — so happy but so shocked — that I almost couldn't suck enough air in to say it out loud.

"Gidge?" I said in a tiny voice. "Is that you?"

CHAPTER 17

didn't wait for her to answer. I didn't need to. It was so obvious.

Her hair was different and so was her style, but behind those great big glasses? Those were Gidge's eyes. There was even something about her voice. The way it swooped up and down. The words she used. It was Gidge.

I screamed, "You came back!"

She staggered into a clothes rack and her hand thumped against her chest. Her mouth bounced as if she had words stuck in her throat, but she didn't blink once.

I'd never been so happy in my life. I tackled her.

Not, like, knock-her-down tackled. *Love*-tackled her. I charged into her and then hung on with my heart pounding and my arms around her belly, just squeezing, squeezing, squeezing her back into my life. The flubbiness of her stomach, the way her arms jiggled, the cracking sound her bones made. The beauty and the bumps. Just like Gidge told me. I'd missed it all so much. Everything was good again.

At least that's what it felt like until she went, "Help me!"

CHAPTER 18

"**H**elp me," she screamed again, only sadder this time. She was shaking and gulping and panting like a dog. "Help!"

"Gidge," I said, "I'm right here! Don't worry! I'm not leaving!"

That just made her scream louder. "Help! Get me out of here!"

"What?! Why?" I screamed back. "Tell me!"

But she didn't or she wouldn't. She just kept going, "Help!" so I did the only thing I could do. I held on tighter. I wasn't ever, ever going to let her go.

That's what I told myself — but then someone grabbed me by the waist and started pulling me away, really, really hard. I knew immediately who it was.

Harris.

Harris, who had already done a pretty good job of making me miserable, was trying to take me away from Gidge.

He was yanking at me and going, "Yardley. Stop. You're scaring her! Geez. Let go, would you? Stop!"

Suddenly, everything crashed together in my head, all the happiness of finding Gidge again and all the scariness of maybe losing her again and all the madness at Harris for butting in just when I was finally getting the only thing I'd ever wanted. I let go of her with one hand and turned — just for a second, not even that — and swatted at him.

That was a mistake.

He gave me another yank and I lost my grip, and I couldn't grab her again because now I too busy fighting *Harris* off. I tried to tell him that this was my business and he should just get out of it and he was ruining everything, but he wasn't listening, he was just trying to out-holler me. By the time I'd got it into my fat head that I was wasting my time — that he was never going to understand, that all I needed was Gidge — she was gone.

Gidge and the envelope were gone.

As in *poof.* I turned around. The shop was empty.

I pushed Harris so hard he banged into the counter, then I ran out onto the sidewalk. I went left for a while and then right for a while, and the whole time my head was spinning back and forth like I was a hungry owl. But there was no one on the street, not a soul, just a dark blue car disappearing around the corner.

I stomped back into the shop with my neck out, my brain sizzling, and my body hurting as if someone had kicked me in the chest and left a giant purple bruise where my heart used to be.

Harris was kneeling on the floor picking something up. I should have been suspicious right away — Harris *never* picked anything up, ever — but I wasn't. I was too mad. He shoved the thing into his pocket and stood up.

"You," I said, and it sounded as mean as I meant it to.

"Me?" As if he was so innocent. "What did *I* do? I was just trying to help."

"Help? You call that helping?"

"Yes! You were freaking the lady out. Didn't you see how scared she was?"

"What are you talking about? I didn't scare her. You're the one who scared her, pulling me away like that. And anyway, she was asking *me* to help her, not *you*."

"Why would she ask you to help? You're the one who attacked her."

"What?! Why would I attack Gidge? I was hugging her!" I huffed out a little laugh and shook my head, so he'd know how obvious that was.

He stared at me. "Sorry. *Who* did you say it was?"

I fiddled with a jacket hanging on the rack beside me. I suddenly felt embarrassed. I didn't know why. It should never be embarrassing to tell the truth.

He took a step toward me. "Did you say 'Gidge'?"

I stood up straight. "Yeah," I said, like it was no big deal. He was going to find out sooner or later.

"Gidge." He put his lips together like he was blowing out a match. He scratched the back of his neck. "Gidge?"

"Uh-huh." I re-buttoned a linen blazer that was done up wrong. "That was her."

"You know she's like, ah . . . dead, right?"

"So? Doesn't mean she wasn't here."

"I think it does, actually."

"What? You never heard of reincarnation or something?"

That stopped him for a couple of seconds.

"Gidge got reincarnated. That's what you're saying?"

"You saw her!"

"I saw someone. Didn't look much like Gidge to me."

I turned my face up to the ceiling and sighed. Did I really have to explain this to him? Some things you just understand or you don't. "Didn't you see her eyes?"

"Yeah. They were terrified."

"They were Gidge's eyes! That was Gidge."

"Oh yeah? So why did she run away, then?"

CHAPTER 19

Harris was really bugging me. Asking me that question as if I was crazy or didn't recognize my own grandmother or something! I wanted to tell him to shut up and leave me alone but then it would sound like I didn't know the answer.

And the worst thing was, I didn't.

I realized I should have asked Gidge while she was alive how she planned to be reincarnated, but how could I? The big problem with her coming back from the dead was that she had to die first, and I never wanted to talk about that. Every time Gidge brought it up, I went *la-la-la-la-la-la-la* until she stopped. I couldn't stand to think about it before, but now I had to.

If the lady in pink was Gidge, then Harris had a point. Why *did* she run away? Why *did* she look so scared? Why *did* she scream when I grabbed her?

There were answers that made sense but I saw them coming and I slammed the door to my brain before they could get inside and hurt me.

Gidge would never do anything to hurt me.

Gidge said she'd come back, and she did. "The world works in mysterious ways, and so do I." She used to say that all the time.

"You want to know why?" I said to Harris now. "Just because — that's why."

I walked back to the counter and got to work.

He followed me. "Because what?"

I picked up the freezer bag of jewelry and started scrambling for something snappy to say back.

"Huh?" he said, as if he'd caught me.

"Because she's trapped in the wrong body." It was the first thing that popped into my head, but suddenly it seemed true. The eyes were Gidge's, the rest wasn't. She was in there looking out. That's why she was so scared.

"The wrong body. You mean like this is a sort of *Freaky Friday* thing?"

"Exactly. Mistakes happen." Gidge used to say that, too.

He nodded in the way people do when they realize something's the matter with you and they aren't going to say it but they want you to know that's what they're thinking anyway. It's very rude.

"I bet it's not that unusual," I said, taking a pair of beaded hoops out of the freezer bag and putting them in the *maybe* pile. "I put my gym gear in someone else's backpack once and didn't realize until I got home that I had the wrong one. You never hear of something like that happening?"

"Yeah. But that's not quite the same thing as picking up the wrong *body*."

"Says who? What do you know about reincarnation?"

"Nothing," he said. "What do *you* know about it?"

"More than you."

"Maybe. But you still didn't answer my question. If it was Gidge, why did she run away from you? If that was really your grandmother and she loved you, you'd think she'd want to stay."

If she loved me.

If!

That was an extremely mean thing to say.

I'm not the type of person to hit someone but I needed to hurt Harris for hurting me, and I was too upset to get any words out, so I hit him. I knew it was bad for my karma, but I didn't care. I kept hitting him and hitting him.

He managed to get me by the wrists, but he couldn't stop me from stomping on his feet.

He was going, "Would you quit it? Quit it! I mean it! You crazy or something?" when we heard the door swing open and Con go, "Harris! What is the matter with you? Stop that immediately!"

"Oh, right. It's *me*. It's all *my* fault. Like *I'm* the one who attacked the lady, not Yardley!"

Harris was leaning toward Con with his hand pointing back at me and his jaw sticking out like he was a caveman or something. I was rubbing my wrist as if it hurt and doing my best to look innocent.

"How come *I'm* always the bad guy around here? You always believe *her*. Just because she's your favorite and always has been ever since she showed up here."

Con went, "Oh, now. You know that's not true. But let's be fair. I walk into the shop and see you grabbing Yardley by the wrists and telling her she's crazy. Let's just say, it didn't look good, my friend . . . I apologize if I jumped to the wrong conclusion." He reached out to pat Harris on the arm, but Harris flicked him away.

Con raised his hands like, *oops, sorry.* "How about we all just take a big breath and then you can both tell me what happened?"

"No, forget it. Let Yardley tell you. She's the only one you're going to listen to anyway."

"Harrissss. C'mon, buddy. You know I —"Harris stomped out of the shop and slammed the door before Con could say anything more.

Con watched him go. "Ugh. Did I just make things worse?" He took off his fedora and slicked his hair back in place with both hands. "I've got to remember to go a little easier on him. Poor kid. He really feels like the whole world is against him these days."

No wonder, I thought. *If you butt your big nose in where it doesn't belong, why wouldn't people be against you? Karma for Dummies.*

I wanted to forget about Harris and go back to thinking about Gidge and how I was going to find her again, but Con had both elbows leaning on the counter now and he was looking at me like he wanted a chat.

"Harris just needs a little TLC," Con said. "He's having a rough time."

Oh, did his *grandmother die too?* I didn't say that.

I said, "Is that why he's staying with you for the summer?"

"Yeah. There are some not-very-nice family things happening at the moment. Harris isn't as mature as you are — heck, who is! — but he's a good kid. He's just lonely and bored and a little mad at the world. He could use a friend. It's hard for him not having his laptop anymore."

"Why not just let him have it then?"

"Can't. Court order."

"Court order?" I kind of choked. "Like, police, judge, handcuffs — that kind of court order?"

"Oh . . . Ahh . . . You didn't know?"

"Know what?"

Con straightened his tie, then looked away, then looked back at me. "Um. Okay. Don't say anything to anyone about this. Especially not Harris. Promise?"

I nodded. Con looked so serious.

"Harris hacked someone's account. Not for money or anything. It was just a . . . youthful misjudgment on his part. Absolutely no handcuffs involved."

"You mean he got into someone's emails or something?"

"It sounds terrible but . . . Look, I'm sure he didn't realize the problems he'd be causing. He shouldn't have done it but . . ." Con fanned out his fingers and made a face.

"But what?"

"Well, let's just say it's complicated." He raised his eyebrows as if I was supposed to understand what that meant, but I didn't. "Things were complicated for me at that age, too. There weren't many boys back then wanting to take costume design in school. Thank heavens I had Ms. O'Hanlon. Gidge was my biggest cheerleader. She was the first person who made me feel like I wasn't weird. I was — wait for it — 'extraordinary.' Her word, not mine, and probably a bit of an exaggeration, but it sure helped."

He shrugged. "I'm just paying it forward. And anyway, I love having Harris around. He can stay forever if he wants. And you can too, of course." He tugged on one of my curls and let it *sproingggg* back, then he looked out the window. "I hope he's okay."

He gave one of those sad, *oh, well* smiles. "A little fresh air might do him good. Give him a chance to calm down. In the meantime, how about you tell me what happened this afternoon?"

He motioned for me to sit in the Barcalounger, then pulled a stool out of the dressing room for himself, and I started talking. I told him about the lady coming into the store and how she'd said she was there to pick something up.

"The package!" Con conked himself on the forehead. "Oops. Sorry! Gidge asked me to leave it at the counter, but it totally slipped my mind."

"What?" That gave me a bit of a shock. "The package was from *Gidge*? You mean, she set up the contest?"

"What contest?"

"The Let Bygones Be Bygones contest."

"Hmm." Con looked confused. "I don't know anything about a contest. Gidge gave me a few letters to send out after she, um, passed . . . and she left that big envelope, too. She said a Mrs. Johnson would come and pick it up. If no one came in by such and such a date, I was free to do with it as I pleased."

"Why would Gidge have given away her green velvet dress?"

"That's what was in the package? I was wondering where that had got to. It was a beauty." Con had drooled over the dress the day we'd brought it in.

I nodded — but then I laughed, because it suddenly hit me.

"What?" he said.

"It's like the Egyptian pharaohs!"

"Not following."

"You know. The way they got buried with all their stuff so they'd have it in the afterlife."

He shook his head. "Getting worse, Yardley."

"Okay, not *exactly* like the pharaohs but, you know. Kinda."

"Explain."

"Gidge *knew* she'd be coming back, so she packed up the dress so it would be ready for her."

"Who'd be coming back? The lady?"

He looked at me funny. Of *course* Con wouldn't get it! Why would he? I didn't at first either.

"Okay. Look. This is going to sound a little weird," I said, "but that's just because you don't know who the lady is."

"It's not Mrs. Johnson?"

"That's what she *said* her name was."

"But it wasn't?"

"Nope. Mrs. Johnson is an alias she used to hide her *true identity*." I dragged that last part out to add a little suspense.

"Would I know who this person is in real life?"

"Oh yeah. Would you ever."

"Yardley. What are you saying?" Con put his elbows on his knees and leaned forward. "Did someone, like, *important* come into the shop while I was out?"

I smiled really big and nodded.

"Who?" Con's not usually the type to bounce, but that's what he was doing.

"Gidge."

"What?" Con went completely still. His mouth didn't change but his eyes did.

"Gidge," I repeated. "She came back."

"Came back?"

"Yes! Mrs. Johnson? Or should I say the *so-called* Mrs. Johnson? That was Gidge. In the shop. This afternoon."

"No." His smile disappeared.

"Yes! I saw her with my own eyes."

"No, honey." He reached across and took my hand. "Yardley. It wasn't Gidge. Gidge is . . ." He opened his mouth a few times, trying for the right word. "Gidge is dead."

"You mean *was* dead." I laughed. "She's reincarnated! You know how she always talked about karma? Well, it worked!

- 103 -

She was standing right here. Right in this very spot. I didn't see it at first because of the way she was dressed, but once I got past the hair and the glasses and the pastel pink . . . It was Gidge. Like, I mean, *totally* Gidge."

Con looked at me for a long time then went, "Umm. Wow. That must have been scary."

"Not scary at all! See?" I pointed at the giant smile on my face. "I'm happy. Or, I mean, I *was* happy until Harris pulled me off her and I lost her. But I'll find her again. I know I will. It was just kind of a shock for both of us. I mean, it was bad for me, but it must have been *really* bad for Gidge." I kind of laughed. Gidge never liked flying, and I figured she must have done a crazy amount of it to get back to me from wherever she'd been. Maybe she was just jet-lagged. Maybe that's why she ended up in the wrong body. It was all coming together.

Con patted my hand and said, "When was the last time you had something to eat?"

"I don't know. Why?" Who cared about food at a time like this?

"I think you've got low blood sugar. You feel dizzy? You look pale. Are you all right? It can be very disorienting."

"I'm not dizzy. I'm just a little, like, wound up because —"

"I bet you'll feel better once you've had a snack." He reached down beside his stool and picked up the bag he'd brought back from his walk. "This is my fault. I forgot to give you guys your snacks. I got you corkscrew fries. I know how much you love them!" He peeked into the bag. "Might be a little cold by now. How about I give them a quick zap?" He was already standing up.

I didn't want corkscrew fries.

I wanted him to believe me, which he didn't.

I wanted Gidge.

But I said, "Yeah, sure." I even went, "Yum!" and squeezed my hands into happy little fists. I tried to act as if he'd convinced me. I didn't want to upset him. I also couldn't listen to any more dumb reasons why I was wrong, because I knew I wasn't. I'd looked into that lady's eyes and Gidge had looked back out at me.

Con seemed relieved. "Hold that thought!" he said and disappeared into the stockroom.

I heard the microwave beep and a couple of seconds later he was back with a bag of steaming fries. I choked down a few so I wouldn't look ungrateful but, soon as he wasn't looking, I put the rest into my backpack.

"Con?" I said. He'd gone to the window to change a burned-out spotlight. "Mind if I leave a little early today?"

"No, of course not. When would you like to go?"

"Like, um, now?"

He looked at me, his face all worried again. "Everything okay?"

"Yeah, yeah, 100 percent!" I told him Mima and Pa just needed me at the theater. I'm not sure he believed me, but Con's not the type to accuse a person of lying.

CHAPTER 21

I was upset when I left Over Easy, but I put on my helmet, got on my scooter and calmed down pretty fast. I always manage to get some good thinking done burning around the city on my scooter. Something about having the wind in your ears seems to clear the brain. That's what Gidge used to say.

I was about halfway to the theater when I stopped being mad at Con. It wasn't his fault he didn't believe me. He knew Gidge, but he didn't, like, *know* know her. He just knew the outside part. I knew the real Gidge, her spirit. She promised she'd never leave me and she wouldn't.

My parents would understand. I suddenly could hardly wait to tell them she was back. I got this jingly feeling in my stomach, and my arms and teeth went all tight. I leaned over my handlebars and booted it.

I stopped a couple of blocks from the theater to pick up some dinner. (Con was right about one thing. I *was* hungry.)

We have a tab at The Nook so I went a little nuts. I got a beetroot salad and a slice of Cap'n Crunch cheesecake for Mima and a Hawaiian pizza for Pa and me to share. I figured it was a celebration so that was okay. While I waited for my order, I sat on a bench outside and fed the leftover corkscrew fries in the bottom of my backpack to pigeons that were hanging around. Gidge and I used to feed the birds when I was little. I imagined us doing it again sometime soon.

"You're in a good mood," the owner said when he handed me the takeout boxes.

"My grandmother came back," I said. "We're having a party!" I shoved the small boxes into my backpack, balanced the pizza box on my handlebars, then headed over to The Hoof & Mouth Theater.

The building it's in used to be an animal hospital. It's a really ugly brick cube, but the rent is cheap and it has lots of parking. I wanted to get my parents together to tell them about Gidge, but when I got there Mima was on the phone in the office begging someone to fix the one and only toilet in the women's washroom before curtain time that night, so I knew I couldn't interrupt. I just put her meal on the desk.

Mima squeezed her phone onto her shoulder with her cheek and checked to see what I'd brought her. She mouthed "Cap'n Crunch!!!" like she was Tigger or something, then went back to begging the plumber. She scribbled the word

"PROPS" and a smiley face with a beard on the cheesecake box, so that's where I went to find Pa.

The props department is in the basement. Gidge used to say it smelled like wet dog and loneliness. It has concrete walls and tiny windows and fluorescent lights that make sizzling sounds just before they burn out. Pa stores the props in the old chain-link kennels nailed to the wall. They're full of crazy stuff like neon-pink suits of armor, giant angel wings, chopped-off heads and a six-foot-tall papier-mâché meerkat folded in half and staring out through the cage with its one good eye. The rest of the room is basically a junkyard — wood, paint, paper, tools, old boxes, building supplies, whatever. It's Pa's happy place.

I could see his legs sticking out from under a giant potted plant. If you didn't know any better, you'd think the pot had fallen from the sky and crushed him. Very Wicked Witch of the West.

I went, "Pa . . . Papa . . ."

No response. The guy's a podcast junkie. I figured he had his headphones on. I knelt down and flapped the pizza lid his way. That usually worked.

"Do I smell . . ." he sniffed a couple of times, ". . . pizza?!?" He slid out from under the pot and his shirt lifted up. Pa's pretty skinny, but his stomach's round and furry, kind of like an enormous kiwi fruit or a baboon belly (regular size).

"Oh, wow. Not just pizza — but Yardley, too," he said, sitting up and slipping his headphones down around his neck. "Bo-nus!"

There's a worktable made out of an old door and two saw-horses against one wall. That's as close as the props department comes to a sofa. I pulled myself up onto it and bent the pizza box open. Pa went to grab a slice, but I was like, "Whoa. Wash your hands." He'd been rolling around on a floor thousands of dogs had peed on.

He crossed his arms, put his hands in his pits and slid them across his T-shirt. "Better?"

"No. Ugh. But fine." Just don't touch *my* side." I scooched two slices toward me.

"Picky-picky." He took a bite. "You're early tonight, Yardbird. To what do I owe the pleasure?"

"I have a surprise."

"Good or bad? Your mother already told me about the toilet."

"Neither. *Excellent.*"

"Oh, well then. Keep talking!"

I put my slice of pizza in the box and inhaled through my nostrils. I wanted to sound calm, but I opened my mouth and "Gidge is back!" came flying out. My bum was clenched so tight I swear I was sitting three inches taller than usual.

"What?" Pa stopped chewing and gawked at me. I could see a mushy orange tennis ball of pizza wedged between his back teeth. "What did you say?"

"Gidge is back. I saw her today."

He put his slice down.

"Gidge." He was clearly in shock. He started chewing again but in slow motion this time.

"I know. I know," I said. "Crazy, right? She came into the shop and I didn't even recognize her. Gidge said her name was Mrs. Johnson and she was wearing pink and her hair was straight, so I was like, yeah, okay, it's just some lady named Mrs. Johnson."

He swallowed. "What do you mean you didn't recognize her?"

"You wouldn't have either! She looked so different. But you know what Gidge is like. She probably planned it that way." I laughed. Just the thought of her trying to trick me. "This so-called Mrs. Johnson said the green dress was hers and I said no, it's Gidge's, and I looked right at her because I was sort of mad — you know, some stranger prancing in and taking credit for it and everything — but then, boom! I looked in her eyes, Pa, and I just knew."

He slid his cap off his head. His hair was so sweaty it stuck to his scalp like ramen noodles. "Is this a joke?"

"No! Would I joke about this?" The look on his face. I started to laugh. "Karma patrol paid off. She's been reincarnated!"

I took a big bite of pizza. I kept forgetting I was hungry.

Pa wiped his hand over his face and down through his beard. He clicked his teeth together a few times, then he scratched his neck and said, "Yardley . . . YaYa . . ."

"What?" My mouth was full.

"That's not the way this works."

"Yes, it is." I picked off a mushroom that had somehow stowed away on our Hawaiian pizza and put it back in the box. "You die and then they check out your karma and your friends' karma and if it's good enough you get to —"

"Who's 'they'?"

I shrugged. "I don't know. Someone up there, or like, wherever. They make sure your karma's good, then they —"

"No, Yardbird. It's not like that."

I wanted to argue, but Harris was right. I *was* a little fuzzy on how reincarnation actually works. I was also a little annoyed that I had to explain it to Pa because, I mean, what did it matter how Gidge got here? She was back. I went, "Pa-ah," but he just barreled right over me.

"Trust me, sweetie. I've been through this before. My dad died when I was twenty-two. I couldn't believe he was gone either. I kept thinking I saw him on the street. I'd spot someone in a jacket like his or with hair like his and I'd run after the guy all frantic and he'd turn around and it wouldn't be Dad. It would be someone else entirely. We all do things like that when we lose a person we love. We don't want it to be true, so our brains keep coming up with proof that it isn't. We can't take the pain all at once so we ease ourselves into it. That's what happened to you. Your brain was just protecting you. A lot of people experience delusions after a —"

"Did you say 'delusions'?"

"Okay, not like 'crazy person delusions,' I just mean —"

"You don't understand." I couldn't believe this was happening. "I didn't just run after some rando stranger on the street! I saw Gidge! I talked to her! Hugged her! It was her!" I wanted to tell him how scared she looked, stuck inside someone else's body, and how I could tell she needed me, but I couldn't. Suddenly I was crying really hard, and I wasn't enjoying it, no matter how much I knew Gidge would want me to.

I was so mad at him. Of everybody — everybody in the whole wide world! — Pa should have believed me. But he didn't. He put his arms around me and held my face against his chest and rocked me back and forth like I was some stupid little kid who'd just found out Santa isn't real. Snot oozed out of my nose. My body wobbled like it was about to explode. My mouth made weird noises.

"Yardbird. Stop it, honey, stop. Please. You're breaking my heart."

I'm breaking *his* heart. What about him breaking mine? Him breaking Gidge's! Not believing she'd come back. Thinking she wouldn't keep a promise! I filled my lungs up with air and held it in until my ribs hurt and I saw stars and the tears stopped. No way I was going to cry if he didn't love Gidge enough to believe me.

"Better?" he said after I'd been quiet for a while. I nodded and sat up straight. I wanted to get away from him. He wiped the wet from my face. His hands smelled like metal and pizza and dog pee too, or maybe I was just imagining that because I hated him so much.

"This might actually be a good time to tell you about a surprise Mima and I have for you."

"What?" I said as if I didn't want to hear it, which I didn't.

"You remember Andreas? Bald guy? Big mustache that curls up at the ends?"

I shrugged, like, *yeah.*

"Well . . . he runs this amazing creative arts camp on a lake just outside the city and —"

"No!" I said, by which I mean *screamed.*

"You haven't even heard what I was going to say."

"I am not going to camp, so forget it." I jumped off the table. "Why would I want to go to camp?"

"For fun, Yardbird. You'll make new friends. You'll —"

"I don't *want* fun. I don't *want* new friends."

"You *think* you don't because you're sad. But that's what you need. That's what Gidge would have wanted for you. To get on with your life."

He didn't know what Gidge wanted. He clearly didn't know anything about her. *I* was the one who saw her. She wanted me to help her. Needed me to help her. I didn't know how, but she did. I saw it in her eyes. She was scared of some-thing, but no way it was me. She loved me. She wanted to be with me *always*. Forever. That's what she said.

"Time heals all wounds," Pa said. "Ever hear that expres-sion? I know that sounds ridiculous right now when we're all still hurting from losing Gidge but it's true, honey. It really is. And getting away helps too. That's why Mima and I think it would a be good idea for you to spend some time in the coun-try. A new environment, new things to do, new people to meet."

"No," I said, but quietly this time.

"You'd love it. I know you would, once you got there. The August session is starting this Saturday and guess what? Andreas had a cancellation, and he said he'd love to have you. He was such a fan of Gidge's and . . ."

Pa just kept talking and talking and talking about the stupid camp, and somewhere along the line I started nodding, and the only reason it wasn't a lie is because I didn't say the words to make it one. No way I was abandoning Gidge. I was staying in the city and I was going to find her and do what-ever she needed me to do.

I'd just let Pa believe he was sending me away. I could hardly wait until I'd show up back here with Gidge. I pictured the two of us, standing right here in the props room. Pa look-ing back and forth between Gidge and me and then stum-bling into the flowerpot in shock, and falling over and breaking the flowerpot into a million pieces. *Told you so,* I thought.

"So, we're good, then?" he said.

"Yeah."

He kissed me on the forehead. "We all miss her, Yardbird. Trust me, there are some days I can barely stand it."

Pa looked away. He was quiet for a while before I realized he was crying.

That made me cry too, because even though I was really mad at him, I didn't want him to be sad.

A second later, I heard footsteps tumbling down the stairs and Mima going, "You guys okay?"

Pa said, "Oh, you know. Just thinking about Gidge." He wiped his face on his sleeve. He didn't want Mima to be sad either.

Mima snuggled in beside us. "That's why I came down. I was thinking about her too."

We leaned our foreheads together and stood there like a sad little teepee. We cried and cried until Pa took out his phone and put on his sixties playlist. "C'mon. Let's dance like Gidge is still here," he said, and I did.

Because she was.

CHAPTER 22

The obvious person to talk to about this was Dead Gidge, but she'd disappeared. I knew it the second I walked into her room that night. Her cloud was gone.

I'd checked all through my head and under the bed and behind the curtains and in The Wardrobe Department and still didn't see-slash-smell her. Maybe it was just that reincarnated beings couldn't be in two places at once, but it still didn't seem fair. How was I going to figure out how to help her without her helping me figure it out?

"What am I supposed to do, Gidge?" I threw one of her sparkly pillows against the wall and it bounced off a Picasso poster and knocked the poo vase onto the floor.

Pa opened the door and stuck his head in. "You drop something?" He was in his boxers and holding a large bowl of granola with two spoons sticking out.

"No. Why?"

Pa looked at the poo vase. Rotten-flower-slime drooled out the top onto the floor. "How did that get there, then?"

I put the vase on the nightstand, wiped my foot back and forth to sop up the slime and shrugged.

Normally, if he'd caught me lying like that he would have said, "Musta been a ghost," and wiggled his eyebrows at me, but he didn't this time. He just said, "Love you, Yardbird. Don't stay up too late," and closed the door.

I flopped onto the bed, my arms stretched out like an exasperated *T*. It reminded me of that trust game where you fall backwards and someone's supposed to catch you.

Gidge had always been there to catch me.

Now I had to do the same for her, even if I didn't know what she needed or how I was going to get it or even if I could. The word *hopeless* appeared in my head.

I let that sink in for a while.

Wrong, I thought.

"I got this," I said out loud.

"Got what?" Pa said from outside my door.

"None of your business. Go to bed." I had work to do.

CHAPTER
23

When I came downstairs the next morning, Mima and Pa were at the kitchen table drinking coffee and eating leftover pizza with their feet stretched out on Gidge's chair, as if she was gone for good and they could use it any old way they wanted. When they saw me looking, they put their feet on the floor and sat up straight.

Pa went, "Yo, YaYa." We'd been really smiley with each other ever since our talk the day before. We were both pretending everything was A-OK. "Whaddaya got on for the day?"

"The usual." It wasn't exactly a lie. I'd been running after Gidge for twelve years and, except for a little break while she was out floating around the universe, that's what I was still doing.

"Is that skirt from our *Teenyboppers In Love* play?" Mima asked. I was wearing a dirndl poodle skirt in lemon-yellow twill, accessorized with my Gidge barrette, a cap-sleeved white cotton shirt and work boots I'd spray-painted turquoise last winter. The paint hadn't stayed on very well but that was okay. The beauty and the bumps. The good and the bad.

"I guess."

"Wow. And you're big enough to wear it now . . ." She pouted at Pa. "Our widdle girl is gwowing up." Pa turned down his bottom lip and they both gazed adoringly at me.

"I'm leaving before this gets sloppy."

"Better run, then." Pa grabbed my skirt and pulled me in for a group hug.

"Ugh," I went, but I didn't really mean it. I hadn't managed to hate him as much as I'd wanted to. I stole a bite of his pizza while they slobbered over me, then I left.

I put on my helmet and got on my scooter. Normally that would have given me a little burst of energy, but I'd had bad dreams all night about Gidge's eyes trapped in someone else's face, and people thinking I was crazy, and me running into my room to get away from them but it wasn't my room, it was camp, and it was full of kids I'd never met all pretending they wanted to be my friends. So I hadn't slept much. And when I'd woken up I'd realized I still didn't know what I needed to do, and that made me even more tired. All I knew was I needed to find Gidge. But how?

We used to watch a lot of cop shows on TV, so I was like, *Okay, what would a detective do?* The only eyewitness was

Harris, so forget *that*. Con wouldn't be happy about me dusting the shop for fingerprints, even if I knew how do it which I didn't. I'd already looked up the name Johnson online and about ten million of them lived around here so that didn't help either. I needed someone to figure this mess out for me.

That wasn't going to happen. I only had me now. Sad but true. I decided to go back to Over Easy. Maybe she'd return to the scene of the crime. I took a big breath and pushed off out the driveway.

When I got to the shop, Con was outside setting up his BOGO sidewalk sale.

"And she arrives in a blaze of glory!" He held two scarves up in front of a mannequin and gave them a little shake. "Which one? Plaid or floral?"

I considered the options for a few seconds then had a brainwave. "Both. The contrast will add a nice pop."

"Genius."

"Yeah. I wish." A genius would have known how to find Gidge.

He tied on the scarves and we stepped back to take a look. We tilted our heads and bit our lips. Something wasn't quite right. I moved the knot to the back of the mannequin's neck so the two ends hung behind. We both liked that better.

Con smiled. "What did I tell you? Genius!" He straightened the shoulder seams on the blouse. "Hey, could you do me a favor?"

I was worried it was going to have something to do with Harris and I wasn't particularly fond of him at the moment, but I said "Sure" anyway.

"I need a showstopper for the Top Ten Tops display. Could you find a mannequin and Gidge her up for me?"

Con didn't really need that. He was just trying to make me happy. "Love to," I said and went inside.

Harris was in his usual spot. He grunted when I said hi.

Grunt away, I thought. I smiled back at him because you never know when karma's watching. Then I got to work.

The storage room was small and full of cardboard boxes and smelled a bit like a basement. I rummaged around and found an old mannequin in the back. She was missing her arms and legs, but I figured if I dressed her right, people would think that was on purpose. I brought her into the shop and set her up on the counter.

I dusted her off while I thought *showstopper*. Usually, ideas come to me like Polaroid pictures. Everything's dark and blank for a couple of minutes, then I give my head a little shake and — *tinkly, tinkly, tinkly* — the outfit just appears in my mind in full color.

But not this time. All I could think about was Gidge. For the first time in my life, fashion didn't seem that important. The only reason I kept going was because I'd promised Con I would.

Okay, I said to myself. *A hat. Find a hat and work your way down from there.*

I grabbed some random ones from the headwear display. A big straw sombrero-ish thing, a bucket hat in highlighter yellow, a tacky-cool plastic visor and a plain navy-blue ball-cap, which I normally wouldn't even consider but I was trying to stay open to inspiration. I plopped the whole armload on the counter in a big heap. The sombrero fell off. I leaned down to pick it up and noticed a piece of paper on the floor.

It was poking out from under a rack.

The rack the lady had been standing beside the day before, when Harris had brought out the envelope holding the green velvet dress.

Little bells started ringing in my head. I didn't know why but I knew they were saying, "Pay attention, Yardley!" I put the sombrero back on the counter and went over to pick up the paper.

It was a note typed on Over Easy letterhead. This is what it said:

```
We're like these ballerinas. We were
always better together. We should
never have let such a little thing
come between us. It's my one regret.
```

And then below, written in red ink, were the words:

```
With my undying love, Gidge xoxo
```

My heart was pounding like rain on a roof. I held the paper to my face. Sniffed in Gidge's cloud. Put her crisscross kisses against my cheeks. Read her words again and again and again. I was so happy, in a sad kind of way.

And then it hit me: "These ballerinas . . ."

What ballerinas?

I checked both sides of the paper. No drawings of ballerinas. I looked under the rack, then under the racks beside it, too. I got on my knees. I found a few dust bunnies, two quarters and a breath mint, but that was about all.

I was just getting up when I remembered seeing Harris do exactly the same thing in exactly the same spot the day before. I'd come back into the shop after running out after the lady and he'd been on the floor, rummaging around. He'd seen me, and shoved something in his pocket. I'd been too mad at the time to bother asking what it was.

I looked over at Harris. He was sitting in the Barcalounger, hunched over his puzzle book like a buzzard. Nothing was different about him, but kind of everything was, too. He was pretending he didn't know I was looking at him, but I knew he did.

Harris was up to something.

CHAPTER 24

Harris was hiding something from me. I was sure of it.

I whammed the bucket hat onto the mannequin's head, shoved her into the first camisole I could find and wound some fake pearls around her neck. *Boom.* Done. Not my most brilliant creation but whatever. I had more important things to worry about. I put the mannequin on the Top Ten Tops rack and strolled over to the Barcalounger, all super casual. I wanted to catch Harris off guard.

"I believe you have something of mine," I said.

"Huh?" He scrunched up his face. "I do?" He looked at his book. He looked at his shoes. He ran his fingers under the seat pillow on the Barcalounger. "Oh . . . is this yours?" He held up his pencil. "It was just sitting on the counter. I thought it was —"

"That's not what I'm talking about, and you know it."

He raised his eyebrows way up and shrugged. "Well, this

is my book and that's the only other thing I've got. See?" He held his arms out to the sides. "Nothing."

"What about the thing you picked up yesterday?"

No answer.

"Under the clothes rack."

He was shaking his head as if he was confused, which he wasn't. He was guilty.

"You were right there." I pointed. "You were picking it up when I came back in."

"Oh . . . Ah . . ." He didn't say anything for a while, so I knew I'd caught him. He went, "That's not yours."

"Yes, it is."

"No, it's not. It belongs to that lady. It fell out of her parcel."

"And that lady's Gidge, and Gidge is my grandmother, so it's mine." I explained it slowly so he'd understand.

He sucked in his breath as if someone was taking a splinter out of his finger. "That wasn't Gidge, Yardley."

"Oh yeah? You think so? Well, look at this." I held up the note. "*With my undying love, Gidge*," I said, tapping her signature. "Now give me the ballerinas."

"I don't have them." He moved his book so it covered his thigh, which was all the proof I needed.

I pushed the book back to where it was before. "So what's that, then?" One of the thirty-seven pockets in his cargo shorts had something in it. I could tell just by looking.

His lips went wiggly.

"I can see it," I said. "You might think my brain doesn't work very well but there's nothing the matter with my eyes."

He sighed and slowly took a crumpled wad of newspaper out of his pocket. It was about the size of an orange.

"You lied to me," I said, taking it from him. "Very bad karma."

"No, I didn't."

I opened the paper. Inside was a little old-fashioned ballerina made out of shiny white china. "What's this then?"

"You said 'ballerinas' with an *s*. I only found one."

I was going to say that loopholes were bad for karma too, but that was his problem, not mine.

I put the doll on my palm and turned her around. She was standing on her tiptoes with one leg bent into a triangle at the knee. She had a hand over her head and the other on her waist. Her hair was painted black and her lips were painted red and she was wearing a white tutu with gold edges. I knew those were the colors even though most of the paint had flaked off.

The air around me went suddenly full of tiny sparkly things. All the sound in the shop disappeared. I slapped my hand over my mouth. "It's a clue!" It just kind of came out. The world turned back on. "Gidge left me a clue so I could find her."

"A clue," Harris said like, *Yeah, right.*

I ignored him. I thought, *Why would Gidge leave me a bal-lerina?* It must have some special meaning. I squished my eyes together really hard so I could think better.

Gidge loved to dance. Maybe it had something to do with that. I tried to picture her spinning around on one toe in a frilly tutu, her hair pulled back into a tight bun, a dainty little tiara on her head.

Couldn't do it.

Yes, Gidge loved to dance, but she was no ballerina. Getting down to the Rolling Stones in a green velvet dress — that was more her style.

I opened my eyes and took another look at the doll.

Red lips.

Black hair.

Gold trim.

Tiny feet.

Tiny hands.

A slightly confused look on her face, but that may just have been because half her mouth had come off.

I was running everything through my head as if my brain was Google and I just needed to type in the right word and the answer would pop up.

Did Gidge ever make a tutu? I didn't think so.

Did Gidge and I ever go to a ballet together? No. I would have remembered.

Maybe the gold on the ballerina was supposed to make me think of jewelry. I thought of the two of us giving away Gidge's earrings in the park that day. Maybe she was at the park now. Maybe I just had to go there and look for Mrs. Johnson, and then all I had to do was . . . I didn't know. How do you get a person out of the wrong body?

"Um . . . Yardley?"

I realized I must have been muttering out loud.

"What?" I answered, but just barely. I didn't want Harris interrupting my thinking.

"You're not thinking of trying to find Mrs. Johnson, are you?"

"What does it matter to you?"

"I don't quite know how to say this . . ."

"But?"

"Mrs. Johnson didn't look like she wanted you bothering her." Harris bared his teeth as if he was embarrassed to have to tell me. "I think she wants you to leave her alone."

"Oh yeah? What makes you the expert?"

"I saw her face. I heard what she said. She wasn't exactly thrilled to see you."

"Well, maybe 'Mrs. Johnson' wasn't. But Gidge will be. Why would she leave me the note if she didn't want to see me? No. Let me answer. She wouldn't! Which is why I'm going to find her."

He sort of laughed.

"I don't care if you don't believe me," I said.

"I believe you."

"So why were you laughing?"

"I wasn't laughing because it was funny. I was laughing more like, you know, uh-oh."

"Uh-oh?"

"Yeah. Like, uh-oh, Yardley's going to track down Mrs. Johnson and it's not going to be good . . . I mean it, Yardley. That lady doesn't want to see you."

"Says *you*. It's not going to stop me. I'm going to find her."

Harris sighed. "Well, okay. If that's what you want to do . . ."

"It is." I really liked how brave that made me sound.

". . . but I'm going with you then."

"What?!" Now *I* was the one who laughed. "Thank you, but no. I'll be fine." I smiled, but not very politely.

Harris said, "Sorry. That's not going to stop me either."

"I'd rather do it on my own, actually." My smile kept getting ruder.

"I'm still going."

"Ah. No, you aren't."

"Then I'm telling Con."

"What?"

He flipped back his hands like he had no choice. "Con wouldn't want you out running after a dead person. He'd probably feel like he had to tell your parents."

"Why do you even want to come with me? Seriously. Why? You're just going to ruin this for me. I don't want you. You can't come."

"I'd better tell him then." Harris grimaced, like, *Hate to do this but . . .*

"You'd better not," I said.

Harris hollered, "Connie!"

I growled, and my hands automatically bent into claws as if I was going to strangle him.

Con called out from his office, "What's up, buddy?"

My hands went from strangling to praying. I dweebered, "Please don't, Harris, please don't. Seriously. Please."

Con could *not* find out about this. He's a super nice guy but I'd seen the look on his face when I told him about Gidge. He'd call my parents. They'd send me to a doctor. They'd send me to camp. Gidge would disappear.

"Please. Harris. Don't."

"Then let me come with you."

"No."

Harris looked me right in my face. "Is that your final answer?"

I stood up really straight and nodded. This was my life, not his.

"Harris?" Con called. "There a problem?"

Harris whispered, "Sorry," to me as if he actually might mean it, and went, "Yeah, Con, there is."

Con poked his head out of the office door. "What's up?"

"Do you know a nine-letter word meaning 'blackmail'?" Harris was a surprisingly good actor.

I turned my back to Con and pretended to straighten out some blouses. I stuck my eyeballs out at Harris, which kind of meant *please* and kind of meant *I'm going to kill you if you say anything*.

"Hmm . . . Gee." Con scratched his chin. "You're so much better at puzzles than I am."

"It's on the tip of my tongue," Harris said, ignoring me and my eyeballs. "You know . . . that word for when you make someone do something by threatening them with something even worse?" He tapped his pen on his forehead and scrunched up his lips.

I squeezed a shirt sleeve in my fist and mouthed "Fine" at him. I turned back toward Con and said, "Would the word be, um . . . EXTORTION?" I counted the letters out on my fingers and wiggled them. "That's nine."

"Bingo." Harris scribbled something in his puzzle book. "Thanks."

"Wow," Con said. "You don't need little old me. You guys make a great team!" I hated how happy that made him, even if it was good for my karma. He went back into his office.

Harris waited until we heard Con's chair squeak into place, then, for the first time since I met him, he smiled at me.

CHAPTER 25

Harris didn't get to smile at me just because he'd won.

I said, "You've got a booger on your lip," which he did, but that's not why I said it. I needed some time to think about this.

He wiped his hand over his mouth.

"Still there," I said, which it wasn't, but I made a little gagging noise as if it was.

I kept saying, "Still there . . . still there . . ." while he wiped and wiped until he finally went, "Aargh," and huffed off.

It took him, like, thirty-two seconds to go to the washroom, figure out I was lying and come back. In that time, I realized five things:

1. I didn't have to put up with this. Harris had no right to butt into my business. He'd already made a mess of things for me once.

2. I didn't need him. Gidge always said I could do anything I put my mind to.

3. But Harris might come in handy. Having a helper with a thing for puzzle-solving could be useful. I was pretty sure the ballerina was a clue. I just didn't know for what yet.

4. The criminal record might come in handy too. I had no idea what had happened to Gidge but I'd do anything I could to get her back. Anything.

5. I didn't have a choice. I had to take Harris with me, otherwise he'd tell Con and Con would tell my parents and that would be that. They'd make me go to camp and I'd lose Gidge forever.

Harris came back from the washroom and went, "What booger? There was no booger. You were just doing that to get rid of me."

"Wow." I clipped a spider brooch to the mannequin's bucket hat. "You really *are* good at puzzles."

He said, "That's not funny."

"Not trying to be. I'm serious. You are. Which is why I've decided to let you help me."

"Thank you." He looked at me suspiciously. "I think."

I rummaged under the counter and threw the phone book

at him. "Would you mind looking in here to find the nearest antique shop?"

"What for?"

"Because the ballerina's old and she's a clue. A person with an antique shop might be able to tell us something about her. I'll be back in a second." I walked past him.

"Where are you going?" he said.

"To talk to Con."

"About what?"

"You," I said, and went to the office.

It probably wasn't good for my karma, but I loved how freaked out that made him.

CHAPTER 26

Con's office was only about as big as your average toilet cubicle. There was an old wooden desk squeezed into one end of the room with an old typewriter on top of it and an old wooden chair with metal balls for wheels and an old black phone with a long curly cord and a white dial with holes for where your fingers go. It took him ages to make a phone call but he didn't care. Con liked doing things his way.

I knocked on the door.

Con spun around in his chair. "Why, Yardley! Fancy meeting you here!"

I was trying to look happy, but I guess I didn't because he saw my face and went, "Harris not bothering you again, is he?"

"No, no. It's just, ah . . ." I twirled the hair on my Gidge barrette. "We were kind of wondering if we could take off for a while this morning?"

"Who's *we*?"

"You know, like, Harris and me?"

"You and . . . and *Harris*?"

"Yeah, um, I mean, if it's not very busy in the shop, I thought it might be fun" — that was a stretch — "if we went out for a snack. We could bring you something back too if you'd like, and —"

Con covered his mouth as if I'd just asked for Harris's hand in marriage.

"Absolutely. Ab-so-*lute*-ly!" He jumped up and whizzed past me. "Harris! You ready to go?"

Harris was at the counter studying the ballerina, all Mr. *CSI* or something. He saw Con come through the door and I guess he must have been afraid Con would notice the ballerina or something because — *bang*! — Harris flopped over the counter as if he'd been shot in the back. A little dramatic but whatever. No way Con could see the ballerina now.

Con said, "Are you okay?"

"Yeah. Why?" Harris lifted his head just enough to move his lips. "Can't a guy relax around here? Geez."

"This is no time to relax! You've got snacks to eat, my friend." Con snapped his fingers. "Chop-chop. Get ready. Just let me grab something for you. I'll be back in a jiffy."

I took the ballerina from Harris and put it in my backpack. Then I got my scooter and helmet out of the broom closet.

Con scurried back in with a twenty-dollar bill folded into

a long V. "Buy yourselves a treat. It's on me!" He started to give it to Harris, then went, "Mmmmm . . . maybe not," and handed it to me instead. He winked. "Just to be on the safe side." He flicked his fingers at us. "Now scat! Vamoose! Go have fun."

He shuffled us out the door and stood on the steps waving farewell, as if we were heading off into some strange and distant land, which we kind of were.

I waited until we were far enough away that Con couldn't hear us, then I said, "You find an antique store?"

"*Yes*. What? *You* don't think I can do anything right either?"

Harris growled and took off without waiting for me to put my helmet on, even though I was the one who'd got him the morning off, not to mention the free snacks. For a few seconds I just stood there, so mad I couldn't move at all then I kicked off and caught up with him.

I went, "Hey. Why are you so grumpy all of a sudden? You were the one who wanted to come with me."

"Who said anything about 'wanting'?" *He* did, but whatever. "I'm trying to help you. I'm trying to make sure you don't do something dumb. You really think I *want* to spend time with you in your weird little outfits and your . . ." He stared at my head. "I don't even know what to call that."

"Six letters. Protective headwear." I wasn't going to let him push me around. "C'mon. I thought you were the puzzle king."

"Yeah, well, bike helmets don't usually have goat horns sticking out of them."

"They're actually ram horns but, since they're plastic and not as authentic as I'd hoped, I'll accept goat horns. Two points for Harris."

"OMG." He squeezed his eyes shut and shook his head. He made a groaning noise like someone trying to lift something really heavy.

"Relax, would you?" I said, which might have been a mistake.

He opened his eyes and bugged them out at me. "You think I'm stupid and I'm not. You think you know everything and you don't. You're the one who needs help around here, not me!"

"Oh yeah? Says who?"

He stormed off before I could finish, which was extremely annoying.

I can't believe you'd do this to me, I said to the Gidge in my head. *First you ditch me, then you stick me with* him?

"You coming or what?" Harris hollered at me from halfway down the block.

A red-haired lady walking by said, "Don't let him talk to you like that."

We both looked at Harris. He was glaring at me with his arms straight down and his hands in fists and his face all maroon and angry.

I went, "Pff! His problem, not mine." That's what Gidge would've said, although she would have meant it nicer than I did.

"Wow." The lady laughed. "Good attitude. Very mature." She gave my helmet a happy little rap and walked off.

I scootered up to Harris and then right on past him. "You coming or what?" (So much for mature.)

Harris spat out about $6.75 worth of swears but he ran after me. I could hear his flip-flops slapping on the sidewalk.

After a while the slapping stopped and the swearing started again. I kept going for a bit but then I stopped too. I turned and saw Harris holding a broken flip-flop and limping along on one bare foot. I put my feet on either side of my scooter and my elbows on the handlebars. I remembered Gidge not being able to keep up. I thought about Barry in the convertible doing a U-ey and coming back for us that day we went to talk to KooKoo. The lawn mower guy from the cemetery driving us to the bus stop. Everybody helping.

I scratched my forehead. I thought of all the reasons this was totally different and how it was Harris's own stupid fault for not even bothering to wear real shoes and how I never wanted him to come anyway. I thought about karma and all the things I'd have to do to make the universe realize I deserved to get Gidge back. Then I turned around and scootered back to get him.

"Hop on," I said.

"What?"

"You move like a two-toed sloth," I said. "I don't have all day. Get on."

For a while, he stood there staring at me like I was a worm that had crawled out of his peanut butter sandwich, but then he sighed and climbed on behind.

"Okay. So where are we going?" I said.

"To 9472 Payzant Road."

"You're sure?"

"Yes, I'm sure."

"You didn't write it down?"

"I didn't need to write it down. I've got a good memory. Can we just go?"

"Hold on to my backpack and just stand there." Pa and I double-rode all the time so I knew I could do it. "I'll push."

Harris was a little wobbly at first and made squeaking sounds every time we went over — I'm not kidding — a *pebble*, but he got used to it. He'd go "Left," or "Right," or occasionally "Stop!!!" as if I was going to crash right into traffic on purpose or something.

"Straight ahead," he said when we got to the corner of Young and Kempt. The road took a big nosedive after the intersection so I was like, "Get ready! This is going to be good!"

We started off at the top of the hill going scooter-fast but pretty soon we hit bicycle-fast, then motorcycle-fast, then full-on racing-car-fast. Harris went from squeaking to making these *whoo-ow-WHOA-ooh* type noises as if I wasn't 100 percent in control, which I totally was.

I was going, "It's okay, it's okay," and it would have been if he'd just relaxed and enjoyed the ride, but he didn't. He grabbed me by the horns and, I don't know, tried to steer me or something, which was so dumb. The only thing he managed to steer was my helmet right over my eyes. Suddenly, it was like I was driving blindfolded.

I'd let go of the handle for half a second and push my helmet up but that would just make us swerve, and he'd grab my helmet harder and push it back down, and I wouldn't be able to see again and we'd swerve some more. I was screaming "Don't!" at him and he was screaming "Don't!" at me and then we were both going "Stop, stop, stop!" which neither of us did until we got almost all the way to the bottom of the hill and then we went flying.

CHAPTER
27

And I mean *flying*! Harris did a major splat on the sidewalk, which must have killed like crazy. I didn't get hurt too bad but that's only because I was wearing my helmet, and also because I landed on top of him. I got off really fast.

"You all right?" I said.

He was lying on the pavement with his mouth open and his arms stretched out and a horn in each hand as if he'd just slayed a ferocious beast or something. He didn't answer.

I was so scared I wasn't even mad he broke my helmet. I didn't like Harris very much but that didn't mean I wanted to smush him to death. Con liked him a lot, plus there was the whole karma thing to think about.

"Harris?" I crouched down and gave his shoulder a little shake.

He groaned.

"You okay?"

He opened one eye, then the other. "You drive like a maniac," he said.

"Oh, ah, thanks." I was pretty sure he'd meant it as a compliment.

"That was insane." He sat up and laughed.

"Yeah, thanks to you! I couldn't see. What were you trying to do, grabbing my helmet like that?"

"Uh . . . survive? I thought for sure we were going to be hamburger for a while there." He chuckled and rubbed the back of his head. "Ow, ow, owwwww." His mouth squished up to his nose and he made this little woodchuck sound with his teeth. "I think I did something."

"Let me look." There was a bump on his head the size of a dumpling. I made a face when I saw it, but I was pretty sure he didn't notice. "Seems okay to me," I said. "Wanna get going?"

I put the horns in my backpack and got on the scooter. "C'mon. Hop on."

"What? And *die*?" He was still laughing. "I don't think so." He stood up and shook little pebbles out of his hair.

"Fine. Suit yourself. You going to walk the rest of the way with one bare foot?"

"Yeah. Why not? It's right there."

He pointed down the side street. There were a bunch of old wooden townhouses and an Ethiopian grocery store and a hair salon and then, just past that, a flat-topped brick building with a big window and a sign that said "Treasure Trove Antiques."

I took off as soon as I saw it. Harris said some bad words, but laughing this time, and ran after me. I skidded to a stop in front of the store, snapped my scooter shut and went inside.

There was a lot of sunshine that day but only two skinny rays made it through the window. They looked like light-sabers. That's how dark the shop was. The furniture was brown and old and ugly and sad and there was so much of it I could barely wiggle my way down the aisle to the counter at the back. Harris was having an even harder time getting through because he had more to wiggle.

There was a little metal dome on the counter with "Ring for service" taped on the side. I dinged it with my palm. A woman immediately came out from a backroom as if she'd been standing there all day just waiting for someone to hit the bell. Her hair was long and gray and so was her face. She had a pair of glasses on the tip of her nose. She said, "May I help you?" but it sounded more like *What are you peasants doing in my store?*

Gidge used to say, "Honey catches more flies than vine-gar." The crankier someone was, the nicer Gidge got. It could be annoying when you were the cranky person — trust me — but it worked. Gidge usually got what she wanted.

I gave the lady my best smile. "I got an antique figurine from my grandmother and I was wondering if you could tell me something about it?"

"Why don't you ask your grandmother?"

Harris went, "She's dead."

"Dead-ish," I said, but I'm not sure the lady heard. She was too busy apologizing. (Even mean people apologize if you say your grandmother died.)

"Well, let's see what you have there." She smiled but she did it fast and she kept her lips together. It was the kind of smile you make when you stub your toe but are trying to be brave.

I reached into my backpack and pulled out the ballerina. I opened the paper and spread it on the counter.

The lady picked the ballerina up by the waist and squinted at her through her glasses. She turned her upside down, studied her feet, her tutu and her face, then put the tiny figurine back on the paper.

"It's not worth a thing."

"Nothing?"

She shook her head and shrugged. "It's a dancer from a music box. Made in China. Probably in the 1920s."

"That was like a hundred years ago!" I said.

"I see we have a mathlete in our midst." Another toe-stubber smile.

"But that's old! She's a genuine antique. She must be worth *something*."

"Uh-uh. No. Wrong."

"How come?"

"Lots of reasons," the lady said. "For starters, it's junk."

"Junk? You're calling her junk?"

"Or crap, if you'd prefer the more technical term. Either would work. Yes, it — not 'she' — is certainly old, but that doesn't mean it's any good. These cheap knickknacks were churned out like popcorn. There are millions of them out there. Every little girl for decades had a music box with a poorly sculpted, poorly painted dancer on it. If I had a nickel for every time someone came into the shop trying to sell me one, I'd be comfortably well off."

"Yeah, well, beauty is in the eye of the beholder," I said, and stood up a little taller.

"You think this is beautiful?" She picked the ballerina up by the head and dangled her in front of me like a dirty sock.

I shrugged. I didn't have to tell her what I thought.

Harris said, "I think she's beautiful."

The lady and I both looked at him in surprise.

"I like the little frilly thing she's wearing." He flicked his finger at her tutu.

The lady snorted, as in, *What do you know?*

"And her hair," Harris said. "And the way her toes point. And . . . ah . . . several other nice things about her too."

"See?" I said to the lady.

She gave a little sniffy laugh. "And do you like how the figurine's broken, too?"

"Broken? Where?" I said.

"The hand." She pointed with the tip of her pen. "Here."

Harris and I leaned in for a better look.

"That's part of another hand, which says to me there were once two dancers. Their hands were joined above their heads. If you had the other ballerina, an expert restorer *might* be able to reunite them and that *might* make it worth something. The double dancers were somewhat rarer, although, if you ask me, why would anyone want twice as much crap as they had before? But, as you say, that's just my opinion. Beauty, eye, beholder, right? And now, if you don't mind, I really should get back to work."

She pushed the ballerina toward me with her pen as if she was worried she might catch something from it.

Harris went, "Excuse me," and flicked his hand at her until she stepped away from the counter. He said, "Thank you," then very carefully wrapped the ballerina in the paper and picked her up like a tiny little baby.

I left the store with my chin up, but my heart was lying in a crumpled heap on the bottom of my soul. Thousands of worthless ballerinas. What kind of clue was that?

CHAPTER 28

"**D**on't listen to her. What does she know?" Harris said. We were on the sidewalk just around the corner from The Treasure Trove.

I said, "She knows the ballerina's not worth anything."

"According to *her*. You saw what was in there. I didn't like a thing in the whole shop. I mean, *yech*. Beauty, eye, beholder, right?"

I sort of laughed. It was nice of him to try to make me feel better, but it wasn't working. All I could think was, *How am I going to find Gidge now?* There were as many old ballerinas as there were people named Johnson, and I didn't have any other clues. I just wanted to be by myself where I could cry if I wanted to.

I said, "Hop on. I'll scoot you back to Over Easy."

"Me back?" he said. "Aren't you coming?"

"I think I'll just go to the theater. Been a long day."

"Oh," he said.

"Oh" is a funny word. It's barely even a word. It's practically just a letter. But you can say a lot with it. It can mean "That's awesome" or "I have no idea what you're talking about" or "I just sat on something pointy."

This time, I was pretty sure it meant something along the lines of "You're just going to dump me off at the shop like I'm some parcel nobody wants."

Harris had been nice to me. It was bad karma not being nice back.

"Unless you want to come too?" I said.

"Nothing else to do." I could tell he was trying not to smile. "Can I drive this time?"

CHAPTER
29

We survived the ride, but just barely. Now I knew why Harris had gone crazy when I was the one driving. Those hills are scary when you're in the back and all you can do is hold on tight and hope you don't die. Harris leaned too far over when he wanted to turn, and he went right through the potholes, not around them, and I was pretty sure he actually tried to hit the curbs just so we'd catch air.

We stopped at a store along the way and blew our whole twenty bucks on candy. When we got to Hoof & Mouth, we called Con from the office and told him we were at the theater and we'd be gone for the rest of the day. He sounded so happy about us not coming back it was almost rude.

The afternoon performance was still on, so Harris and I went downstairs to the props room and just hung out. It was something normal kids would do. It was weird.

"OMG. I thought we were roadkill when we went over

that bump on Robie Street. Did you see the look on that lady's face when we passed her car?" Harris laughed. "Hysterical. You know how pug dogs' eyeballs can pop out when they cough? That's what she reminded me of. A coughing pug." He made a pug face so I'd know what he was talking about, then he picked up a pink spear left over from our production of *Julia Caesar* and clanged it against the metal kennels just because he liked to make noise.

"Shh!" The props department was right below the stage and our soundproofing sucked. I'd already told him that a bunch of times. "Just eat this and be quiet, okay? Please?"

Harris was still hungry even after all the candy we bought so I'd gotten us two big buckets of popcorn from the concession stand. (That's what Pa calls the rickety table he set up in the lobby to sell snacks. Sounds better than it is.) Harris had already wolfed his popcorn down, so I slid my bucket across the worktable to him and went back to gluing my horns back on.

To make them stick, I had to hold them in place for five minutes. While I waited, I stared at my helmet as if it were a crystal ball and tried to figure out what the heck Gidge was up to. Why would she leave a green velvet dress for her reincarnated self? What's the point of a broken ballerina? Why had she run away from me?

Harris went, "Good thing there were no police around to

see us. How freaked out would we have been? Some big cop with his weapon out going, 'You with the horns! Freeze!'" That made us both laugh.

I wiped off a little blub of glue. "Yeah, last thing you need is to get in trouble with the cops again."

I bit my lip, but it was too late. Everything went slow and quiet for a second, kind of like when a glass drops and you're waiting to see if it breaks.

Harris's face went blank. "Con told you."

I'd promised Con I wouldn't say anything. Gidge would be so mad if she knew I broke a promise. Karma wouldn't like it either.

"No . . . I mean, yes, but, like, not really." I almost smiled but then changed my mind. I didn't want Harris to think I was enjoying this. "He just said you got in some trouble."

"*I* got in some trouble?"

"Yeah, but that's all he said." I thought that would make it better, but Harris snorted so I knew it didn't.

"Not *why*? Not who *else* got in trouble first?"

"No. He just said you weren't allowed to use the internet."

Harris shook his head and went, "Ha!" but not as if it was funny. "It's always my fault." He picked up a pair of Pa's pliers and cranked them open and closed a few times.

Neither of us said anything for a while. Then he said, "That's why I got mad at you."

"Mad at me? When?"

"On our way to the antique store."

I'd forgotten about him storming off like that. "Why? What did I do?"

"Nothing. You never do. You're Miss Perfect. That's why Con gave you the money, not me. I'm the one who's always screwing things up." He shrugged and smiled as if it wasn't a big deal, which it obviously was.

"That's not true," I said.

"Oh yeah? So why didn't he give it to me then?"

I went, "Umm . . ." and tried really hard to come up with something.

"Wow. I'm actually right for once!" Harris said.

He picked up the bucket of popcorn and shook it at me, like, *Have some.* I took a handful and said, "Thanks."

"For what? It's *your* popcorn."

"I meant thanks for coming with me."

He threw a kernel in the air and caught it in his mouth. "It was fun. Better than Swiffering the floor again or watching you and Con drool over, like, pantaloons or something."

I laughed. "*Pantaloons?* What are you talking about?"

"I dunno. I mean, like, fashion stuff."

"Such as pantaloons." I couldn't even say it without laughing. "The last person to wear pantaloons was some pirate in, like, 1562."

"Exactly. Tell me you don't want a pair of pantaloons."

We cracked up at that because it was totally true and there was no way I could pretend it wasn't, even if I tried to act like I didn't by throwing popcorn at him. He went, "You do so!" and threw it back at me, and I threw some more at him.

And that's when this goofy voice went, "Hey! What do we have here?"

CHAPTER 30

It was as if we'd been caught doing something we weren't supposed to. Harris and I both froze, then we gulped, then we turned slowly toward the sound.

And there was Pa, leaning against the doorway, dressed like an enormous housefly. The bibbly-bobbly antennae, the bulgy eyeballs stuck on the side of his head, the massive wings — the whole mortifying shebang.

"Why, don't you two look like you're having fun!" he said with a big smile. "Yardbird, aren't you going to introduce me to your friend?"

I went, "Ahhhh . . . ," by which I meant, *Please leave immediately.*

I did the angry Houdini eyes at him and everything, but Pa's not really good at picking up hints, especially when he doesn't want to. He positively *bounded* toward us with his big thorax-y thing splopping along behind him like a giant diaper.

"I'm Fred. Yardley's dad." He grabbed Harris's hand with his plastic pincer and shook it as if he was trying to snap a kink out of a garden hose. "Let me guess. You must be Con's nephew. I've heard so much about you!"

Harris had to know that couldn't be good. It's not like we'd been friends up till now.

"Pa," I said, as in, *Pleeease.*

"Oh, and here's Yardley's Mima!" he said, because now she'd shown up too.

No bounding for her. Mima had to tippy-tap in because the earthworm costume she was wearing was skintight and went right down to her ankles then trailed along behind her like a big raw sausage. The costume was pale pink and so skimpy you could actually see her belly button through it. This didn't stop her from hugging Harris, despite the fact she'd never actually met him and he's twelve and wouldn't want to hug anyone, let alone a skinny, basically naked, middle-aged woman attached to a giant sausage.

"You and Yardley enjoy yourselves," she said, giving his hair a little muss. "I've got to drag Fred back to the ladies' room." She scrunched up her nose. "Toilet problems."

Pa scrunched up his nose too, then looked at us and went, "S'cuse me," in this little kid voice, "I need to go to the baffroom." He picked Mima up and pretended to fly away. He no doubt thought this was going to be much funnier than it actually was.

My face was very hot. I'm pretty sure that was the first time in my life I'd ever blushed.

"Well, that was embarrassing," I said.

Harris didn't say anything.

"Parents, right? Ha ha." I was just making it worse.

He shrugged. "Yeah, well . . . at least you have them."

I blushed for the second time in my life. Gidge always used to say, "Whenever you feel sorry for yourself, just look around and see what other people have to deal with. You'll be glad all you have are your own little problems." Then she got cancer. Nobody's problems were worse than mine after that.

Or at least that's what I used to think.

"You don't have parents?" I said.

Harris picked at his nails. "My mother's gone and I don't have a father."

"Oh. Sorry."

"Whatever." He was blushing now too, or maybe he was trying not to cry. It was hard to tell because he wouldn't look at me.

"Is that why you wanted to help me find Gidge today? Because you lost someone too?"

"Sorta."

"I'll help you find them!" I said. "I mean, after I find Gidge. She'll probably be able to help us too because she knows more about reincarnation than I do. Probably more than anyone does! I mean, after this and everything."

Harris said, "How do you know you're even going to be able to find Gidge?" which was kind of a negative thing to say, but I didn't mind because I knew he wasn't feeling his best right then.

"I was worried after the antique store today. Like, what that lady said about the ballerina being cheap and worthless and ugly and everything? That really hurt my feelings. But you know what I just remembered? The note. Maybe the ballerina was decoration, like the toy with the Happy Meal or something, and it's actually the note that's important." I got the paper out of my backpack. "Maybe there's a clue in here and I just missed it."

"Like what?"

"I don't know. You're the puzzle guy. I bet you can find something."

I stood beside him and we both read the note. Gidge always loved Boggle and Scrabble so I thought maybe it was a scrambled word kind of thing. I moved the letters of "ballerinas" around in my head. I got "slab nailer" and "rain labels" but neither of them made any sense to me or to Harris.

He said, "There is one thing I noticed, though . . ."

"What?" I sounded calm but my feet went a little crazy.

"She didn't start the note with 'Dear Yardley.'"

"So?"

"Yeah, well . . . are you sure the note's for you?"

"What? Of course I'm sure. Why are you saying that?"

"It didn't have your name on it."

"So? The other one didn't either. It had 'Greetings, Earthling.' What? So you think that letter was for some other random earthling too?"

"No, your name was on the envelope. This one fell out of a package with someone else's name on it, and you just happened to be the one to find it."

"Just *happened* to be the one to find it?!? Oh. Come. On." I read the note out loud: "'We're like these ballerinas. We were always better together. We should never have let such a little thing come between us. It's my one regret. My undying love, Gidge.' Who else would it be for?"

He shrugged. I sulked. After a while he said, "What little thing came between you?"

I laughed in the way you do when you want to show how ridiculous someone is being. "Death! Geez. Get with the program, would ya?"

"That's a little thing?"

"For Gidge it was."

"Hmm," he said.

"Hmm" is kind of like "oh." It can mean a lot of things, such as *Let me think . . .* or *Amazing!* or *I don't believe you but I'm not going to say it out loud because then you'll get mad at me.*

That's what it meant this time.

I folded my arms. "Who else would she write it to? Con? No. It was at Over Easy, so it wouldn't be for Pa or Mima. Who was it for, then? You? You don't think it was for you, do you?"

"No."

"So, who?"

"That lady. The one in the pink dress."

"First of all, it was a suit, not a dress. And second of all, that lady was Gidge. Or at least the body's she stuck in. That's why she said 'Get me out of here.' She's come back, and she's in the wrong body, and she needs me to find the lady in the pink so I can rescue her. I already told you that."

He nodded, so I thought we were done, but then he said, "How are you going to rescue her?"

I gave a little snort. "I've got a plan," I said.

Harris didn't need to know my plan was to make it up as I went along. That's what Gidge used to do. She was a big believer in happy accidents and the power of positive thinking. Jump on the bus without knowing which way it was going. Throw the orange scarf on with the purple pants. Say yes to something then figure out how you're going to do it later. She'd say, "What's the worst that can happen? It'll be a fabulous success or a glorious failure. Who cares!" Then she'd dive right in.

Harris went "Hmm" again. This time it meant, *You don't have a clue what you're doing and it's never going to work.*

That was all I needed to hear. Gidge used to say, "People who believe something *can't* be done need to get out of the way of people who believe it *can* be done."

"I think you should go," I said.

"What?"

"Leave," I said. "Now."

"Why?"

"I don't need your help finding Gidge. I can do it myself."

He looked at me for a second, then he said, "That lady doesn't want to see you, Yardley. Trust me. I know what a person looks like when they don't want you around."

"You do?" I said. "Does it look like this?" And then I made the meanest face I could at him.

CHAPTER

31

"**K**nock, knock! Room service for Ms. Yardbird O'Hanlon!"
I groaned and peeked out from under my pillow.
Pa and Mima were sticking their heads in through the crack
in my door, one on top of the other, as if they were in a play
and doing it to be funny.

I pulled the pillow back down over my face. "What time is it?"

"Time to go to Over Easy! You're going to be late." Pa
pounced on me and tickled my ribs, which I hated at the best
of times, and this was not the best of times. I swatted him away.

"I'm not going," I said.

"Had a little too much fun last night, did you?"

"Ha," I said. Fun? With Harris? He'd made me laugh a
little bit at first, but so what? He didn't believe me. He didn't
understand me. No one did.

Except Gidge. She was the only, only person I could ever
trust. The only, only person who made me *me*. I thought about

the rest of my life without her and it was like looking at a big empty store. Nothing on the hangers. Bare-naked mannequins. No lights. No people. The same dumb song playing over and over on the speakers, so even if you wanted to go there you couldn't because it would drive you crazy and you'd be better off all by yourself in your own stupid room, never seeing anyone else ever again.

I rubbed my eyes like I was trying to get the sleep out of them, not the tears, and sat up. That was the only way my parents were going to leave.

"Sleepy girl," Mima said and kissed my head. She clamped Gidge's breakfast tray over my legs. There was an orange cut in one long spiral, three pieces of cinnamon toast with extra brown sugar and a cup of milky tea in a vintage cup that said "Property of Bayport Home for the Criminally Insane." My parents at least knew what I liked. I may have smiled slightly.

"That's more like it," Mima said. "I've got a rental car today to pick up some more of those plastic anteaters for the show tonight, so I can drive you if you like."

"That's okay," I said, unrolling the orange section like a spiky ribbon. "I'll take my scooter."

"Put it in the car. Your friend will be wondering where you are. It's almost nine."

I was just about to say, "What friend?" when Pa went, "Oh,

and by the way . . ." He sat on the edge of the bed and I had to grab my tea to keep it from spilling. "Mima and I have been chatting."

I glared at him. "Is this about that stupid camp again?"

"Yes."

I bent my head back and breathed brain-fire at the ceiling. Camp. As if I didn't have enough problems.

"Now, now . . ." Pa was doing that jokey thing he does when something bad is happening and he's trying to pretend it isn't. "You didn't even wait to hear what we have to say!"

"Anything you have to say about camp is not going to be good." I attacked the orange with my teeth as if I was a predator and it was my victim.

"Oh yeah? What if we say we changed our minds?"

"What?" I put the orange back down on the tray. "Changed your minds?"

He grinned and nodded. I looked at Mima. Ditto.

"You mean I don't have to go to camp?"

"You make it sound like we were trying to punish you!"

"Yeah, well," I said.

He waved that off. "You would have loved it, once you got there, but . . . what's the point now? We just didn't want you to be lonely. You seem to be having so much fun with Harris, it doesn't seem right to drag you away. We figured if you're happy helping out at Over Easy, you should stay. What do you think?"

"I think 'yay'!"

"Awesome!" Pa stood up and I had to grab my tea again. "Well, you'd better get a move on, Yardbird. You're going to be late! Wouldn't want you to get fired and have to go to — ugh — *camp* . . ." He pretended he was being dragged off to a fate worse than death. *"No! No! You can't make me!"* Mima pretended she was a cop and swung his arm behind his back and marched him out. I pretended to laugh.

It wasn't until the door closed that I realized one of the pieces of cinnamon toast had disappeared, but I wasn't even mad. I didn't have to go to camp. I'd have more time to find Gidge.

I could put up with Harris until then.

CHAPTER
32

Mima dropped me at the corner just before Over Easy. I kissed her goodbye and got my scooter out, then stood on the sidewalk for a while staring at the sky. I was worried about going into the shop. I felt bad about Harris's parents, and I knew karma would be expecting me to be extra nice to him because of it, but I didn't want to. I couldn't. The truth was I didn't like Harris very much and I couldn't make my face pretend that I did.

Con must have known something was up.

"Wow. Snazzy outfit," he said after I'd finally made myself go into the shop. I was wearing a strapless teal taffeta dress over a plain white T-shirt, the laughing monkey neck-lace, striped knee socks, silver platform Mary Janes and, of course, my Gidge barrette. A bit fancier than usual but not quite worth the "Woo-hoo!" he gave it. "The color's great on her, isn't it, Harris?"

"Yeah." Harris didn't even look up from his puzzle.

Con whispered, "Sorry," but I just shrugged.

We were having our Retro Prices Sale that day so the shop filled up pretty fast. I got so crazy busy helping customers that I barely had time to think about Gidge, let alone Harris.

Around two, Con sent Harris out to pick up the mail from the post office. He came back with the usual bundle of bills and flyers and small packages. Things had slowed down by then. We only had one customer in the store, and she was just browsing. I was standing at the counter trying to glue an eyelash back onto a mannequin head. It was long and wiry and kept sticking to my fingers like a bashful spider. Con stood beside me, humming as he sorted through the mail.

"Well, Yardley," he said. "What do you know? Another missive from your not-so-secret admirer!"

He waved an envelope at me. It looked like squished Kleenex and had a big red lipstick kiss on the back.

I squealed and slapped the eyelash onto the mannequin's forehead. I grabbed the letter and scurried into Con's office to read it.

I sat in Con's twirly chair and *gazed upon* the envelope. That's what Gidge always did when she got a present. She *gazed upon it.* The ribbon, the paper, the handwriting on the little tag — she wanted to take it all in. Make the most of the experience. I ran my fingers over my name typed on the front. I pressed the lipstick kiss against my cheek. I sniffed the envelope for signs of her cloud. It was very faint, but I was pretty sure I could smell it.

When I couldn't stand the excitement anymore, I gently, gently, gently peeled open the flap at the back. Lipstick got on my fingers. I pulled out the card, smoothed it open on Con's desk and read.

Greetings, Earthling!

I know you're sad but that's because you've been looking for me in the wrong places. I escaped from the lady in the pink suit. If you want to see me now, go to one of my favorite places. You choose. I'll meet you there.

Love,

Gidge

PS Ask Con if Harris can come. Con will be glad to get rid of him for a while.

PPS Sorry about the green dress and the ballerina. I didn't mean to confuse you.

I ran out of the office.

"Harris!" I yelled. He jumped. "Want to go somewhere?"

"Ah, sure? When?"

"Like now." I went to grab my scooter from the broom closet. "I mean, if that's okay with you, Con?"

I totally expected him to say yes. I mean, why wouldn't he? But he went, "Um, sorry, Yardley. Any other time, but Harris is busy, I'm afraid. In fact, his ride's here."

Harris didn't move.

"C'mon, buddy!" Con sounded suspiciously cheery, even for him.

I looked over at Harris. His lips had gone skinny and he was sort of pink around the eyes.

"That's okay," I said. "We can go tomorrow."

"Good plan! You guys can take all afternoon off tomorrow. Do whatever you want. You deserve it! But better get a move on now. Not nice to keep people waiting."

Harris went, "No, Connie. Pleeease. Do I have to?"

Con said, "It'll be fun!" which is what adults always say when it isn't going to be. I almost felt sorry for Harris. He dropped his book on the floor and schlumped over to the door.

"Looking good, buddy!" Con said. Harris huffed something that I didn't hear but which was probably not very nice, then he slammed the door on his way out. I scurried over to the window to see where he was going.

Con came and stood beside me. He rubbed something off my cheek with his hankie. "Lipstick," he said. "Wow. The kiss is still fresh!" He folded his hankie up so the lipstick didn't show and put it in his breast pocket. We both turned and looked out the window.

There was a car parked at the curb. A man was standing on the far side by the driver's door, leaning his elbows on the hood. He was tall and kind of chunky. He took off his ballcap and waved it when he saw Con and me. We waved back. Harris got in the car and slid down into the seat as if he'd melted.

"Who's that?" I said, even though it was none of my business.

"Harris's dad."

"Harris has a father?!?"

Con pulled back his chin and looked at me. "You sound surprised."

"He told me he didn't. I thought his dad died or something."

Con's shoulders slumped. He watched the car until it disappeared around the corner, then he said, "He does have a dad. Just not the one he wants, I guess."

CHAPTER 33

The boll weevil, a.k.a. Elsie Leung, was sick that night so Mima and Pa asked if I'd fill in for her. She only had two lines in the play. One was "But I'm a vegetarian!" which Pa seemed to think was hilarious, and the other was "Dust to dust," which she croaked out just before she rolled over and died. I'd have to lie there on my back with all six of my legs up in the air until the curtain fell but whatever. I had lots of stuff to think about.

Like Gidge's letter, for instance.

I wasn't surprised when she said to look for her in her favorite places. I'd heard her say that before, back when she was alive the first time. It was after one of her chemo sessions. She'd arrived at Over Easy looking terrible. (Sometimes the chemo made her throw up. Sometimes it just made her wish she could.) Con had shooed Harris out of the Barcalounger so she could sit down, but she was like, "No, no, no! You don't have to make such a big fuss about me. I'm not going anywhere!"

For a second, I'd thought that meant she'd gotten good news at the hospital. Like this had all just been a terrible mistake and she was 100 percent okay and she wasn't going to die and we wouldn't have to sell her clothes and we could go back to just being us again and happy. But then she started saying that she'd always be with us, and my insides collapsed. I knew where this was going. She was back on her whole spirit-lives-on thing. She started talking about how soon she'd be floating in the universe and we'd go to one of her favorite places and just know she was there with us. Feel her in the air or something. As if virtual Gidge on mute was going to be as good as the real thing. I just went *la-la-la* in my head and started sewing a button onto a vintage bowling shirt. Con and Harris could keep listening to her if they wanted, but not me.

The new letter, though, made it sound like I really would find her. As in, actual Gidge. Human Gidge. Back on Earth. In my heart, I'd always known she wouldn't leave me. She loved me too much to do something like that.

Which made me think of Harris.

Lying there on the stage while my parents pranced around in bug clothes, I couldn't stop thinking how bad his dad must be.

I kept picturing Harris in the shop that afternoon, practically begging Con not to make him go with his father. That's what I'd been like about camp! But that's normal. Who would want to be stuck in the woods with a bunch of strangers gluing macaroni onto tin cans? No one. But hating your parents that much? That would be terrible. Seriously. I'd rather be a dead boll weevil.

No wonder Gidge asked me to take Harris with me. Things were even worse for him than they were for me, and that was saying something.

CHAPTER 34

I woke up the next morning and thought, *KooKoo!*

I remembered what we'd talked about the day we went to visit her at the cemetery, and I suddenly knew where I'd find Gidge.

I got dressed — tiger-print capris, a cropped Dora the Explorer T-shirt and sneakers with gold laces I'd snitched from the props department — then I went into the kitchen and emptied the swear jar into my backpack. I got Gidge's scooter and helmet out of the garden shed and strapped them onto my back. I told Mima and Pa I might be late. Harris and I were going to do something that afternoon.

I headed off to Over Easy. For the first time in forever, I felt happy.

Harris got in late and wouldn't look at me, so I didn't have a chance to be nice to him the way I'd planned. I got to work, steam-pressing some plaid maxi skirts that had just come in for fall.

At around ten-thirty, Con popped out of his office and said, "Hey. Can I get you two to clear out the swimwear section and set up the Sweater Weather display? It'll give me a chance to take care of some paperwork."

I said, "Sure."

Harris said nothing.

Con waited a couple of seconds then went, "Yoo-hoo! Buddy. Can you give Yardley a hand? . . . Harris?"

Harris kind of sighed. "What do you want me to do?"

"Swimwear goes here." Con handed him a cardboard box. "Neatly, please. The sweaters are in the back. I'm sure Yardley will be able to figure out how to make them look nice."

My brain winced. *Miss Perfect*, I thought, and I bet Harris did too.

As soon as Con left, I walked over to the swimsuit rack and started clearing it out. Harris followed me.

I unhooked the strap of a one-piece that had gotten tangled up in the hangers. "You know that letter I got from Gidge yesterday," I said. "Which, before you say anything, was to *me*. For *sure*. It even had my name on it."

"I know. I saw." He put the box on the floor and took a bikini bottom off the rack. "Ewwww. I hate even touching these things. It's like touching someone else's underwear."

"Then don't. I'll do it."

He turned his face away and handed me the bikini bottom.

I found the matching top and arranged them in the box.

"I think I know where to find Gidge," I said.

"Oh yeah? Where?"

"The letter said I should go to one of her favorite places. That's where she'd be."

"Hmm."

"Hmm, what?" He sounded like he didn't believe me again.

"Nothing. I just remember her saying that to us once."

I kind of laughed. Who knew Harris actually listened to the rest of us talk? He always seemed so bored. "She said it a lot, actually." I shrugged. "I don't know why I didn't think of it before."

"So are you going to go look for her?"

I bugged my eyes out at him in a jokey way as in, *Please!*

"Yeah, okay, obviously, I guess. But, I mean, *where* are you going to look? What was her favorite place? Do you know?" He seemed a little awkward. He took a mannequin by the neck and twisted her head backwards.

"Stop," I said. Then, "Please," in a nice voice. Karma was going to be more important to me than ever. I turned the mannequin's head the right way and made him hold the box so he wouldn't be tempted to do it again. I went back to folding bathing suits.

"I wasn't exactly sure at first. You know Gidge. She has so many favorite places. She likes everything. Scoops Dairy Bar for key lime fro-yo. The Salvation Army for secondhand stuff.

Any toilet when she really has to go." That made me laugh. "She'd come flying into the house after we'd been out all afternoon and race into the bathroom without even shutting the door. I remember her giving this big happy sigh and going, 'Ah! There's nowhere I'd rather be right now.'"

Harris didn't actually say "Ugh," but I got the feeling he was thinking it.

"Sorry," I said.

He gave his head a little shake as if it didn't matter. "So did you try the bathroom, then?"

"No. That's only her favorite place *sometimes* . . ."

"So where then?"

"We were at the cemetery once. Gidge and me. And she was saying how she's always loved roller coasters. How they're like life." I pulled out a blue one-piece bathing suit with a rose appliqued to the hip. I noticed the elastic was coming loose at the leg hole. I put it aside to ask Con what to do with it.

"Like life? How?" Harris said.

"Yeah, you know . . . The way roller coasters go really far up and really far down. The way they can be super fun and super terrifying at exactly the same time. Gidge likes that. She and KooKoo — that's her friend who died — they used to go to the one on the waterfront. I was thinking we could start there. If we don't find her, at least we could get some cotton candy."

I took the box of bathing suits from him and brought it to the counter. He followed me. I closed the top and wrote "SWIMWEAR" and the date on the side in Sharpie.

He went, "So why are you telling me?"

Gidge always used to say, "Honesty is the best policy, unless it's too *much* honesty." I figured telling Harris that Gidge wanted me to take him would be too much, so I just said, "Wanna come?"

"When?"

"Today?"

He shrugged and said, "I guess," but he smiled so I knew he really meant *Yes.*

Harris went back to his puzzles and I got the Sweater Weather display ready. I dressed the mannequins in turtlenecks and cardigans, then cut up a bunch of yellow and orange construction paper and made hats that looked like big piles of leaves on their heads. Con loved the display — but not as much as he loved the idea of Harris and me going to the amusement park together. He dinged open the cash register and tried to give us some money, but I held up my backpack and gave it a shake. "Don't need it." The coins jingled. "I'm loaded!"

I gave Harris Gidge's scooter and I got on mine and we went to the waterfront. It started to drizzle on the way, but I didn't care. It could have poured buckets and I wouldn't have cared. I was going to find Gidge there. I was sure of it.

The amusement park cost twenty-four dollars for the two of us which left exactly seventy-five cents in swear-jar money. (So much for the cotton candy.) The man at the entrance clipped bracelets onto our wrists and said, "Welcome to Harborview Amusement Park," without even looking at us. He sounded like a robot. I don't think he liked his job very much.

The place smelled like hotdogs and buttered popcorn and mud. People in charge of the game booths had their hoods up and were sitting on stools, smoking or sleeping or (this one guy anyway) clipping their toenails. The prizes hanging on the outside of the booths were all covered up with big plastic sheets to keep them dry. Water was pooling on the seats of the Tilt-a-Whirl. Everything was gray.

"Boy," I said, looking around. "Hardly anybody's here."

"Yeah. Good thing people still get divorced."

"What does that have to do with anything?"

Harris jerked his chin at a guy carrying a giant pink teddy bear. A boy about our age was schlumping along behind him, checking his phone. "Why do you think that man's here?"

"I don't know."

"Because he's divorced and it's his day to have the kid." Harris obviously knew what he was talking about. "Who else would come in this weather?"

I was going to say Gidge. She would have come. She loved

the rain. She saw the good in everything. But that would have just been rubbing it in. I had the most wonderful person in the world, and Harris had a dad who only came to pick him up because he had to.

"We don't have to stay long. There's the roller coaster." I pointed down the lane to the far end of the amusement park. "We'll just find Gidge then we can go."

"Sure. Whenever." Harris leaned in close. "Um . . . Is she here, do you think? Can you feel her — you know — spirit?" He kind of whispered, as if he'd just spotted someone at a mall he thought might be a celebrity.

I didn't know. I went totally quiet. I thought I should probably be feeling kind of tingly, like in the movies when something magical happens and there are sparkly lights and music that sounds like notes tumbling down stairs. I breathed in as deep as I could. I looked around, ready to see/feel/hear/sense something — but all I noticed were a few sad, wet people and lots of stuffed toys no one was buying.

"I don't think so," I said. "But maybe I'll feel something when we're closer to the roller coaster."

"Well, what are you waiting for, then?" Harris gave me a little push and we ran.

We were panting hard by the time we got there. "For two, please," I said and held out my arm for the guy to scan my bracelet. He squinted at me for a couple of seconds then made me stand next to a big ruler to see if I was tall enough to get on. He put his hand flat on my head and checked.

"Nope. Sorry. Try the Ferris wheel. You're half an inch shy for this."

"No, she isn't." Harris fluffed up my hair. "See?"

The guy said, "That ain't how it works." But there was nobody else on the whole roller coaster and we kept going, "C'mon. Pleeeease?" so he said, "Ah, what the hell," and jerked his head toward the next car. We sat down and he clamped us in with a metal bar. The roller coaster made a grinding noise and inched forward.

A couple of minutes later two more people got on behind us. The guy had a beard and was wearing a hoodie, and as soon as he sat down he folded his arms and closed his eyes like he just wanted to sleep. The girl was tall and thin with long straight hair and bangs that covered her eyebrows. She looked like she worked at a cool restaurant or sold homemade stuff on Etsy. I smiled at her. I thought, *I wonder if she's Gidge?* but she didn't smile back. She poked the guy hard with her elbow. He opened his eyes and they started to whisper-fight. I turned away. That definitely wasn't Gidge. She was a lover, not a fighter. She used to say that all the time.

After a while the roller coaster started to move. It was slow but noisy. While it crawled up the hill, I told Harris about Gidge and me going to the cemetery, and how she'd said if she hadn't decided to give her body to the medical school, she would have liked us to shoot her remains off the roller coaster.

His eyes went huge. He said, "You mean, like, just throw her body off the roller coaster?"

"No!" I said. "What do you think we are? Her ashes, you dodo!" And I know that's gruesome and horrible and it was my grandmother he was talking about, but when we realized what Harris had been thinking, we started to laugh really hard. I always hated it when Gidge made jokes about dying but there I was, laughing my head off about it, and so was Harris, as if we were friends or something.

I knew that would make Gidge happy, so it seemed okay to do it.

Better than okay. Good.

Great.

Probably even fantastic. In fact, it felt like the Gidgi-est thing ever, laughing like that. Like something she would have done herself.

And then I thought, *Maybe she did.*

Maybe she's here with me now.

I looked at Harris, laughing his head off on the roller coaster with me and I thought something even weirder. *Maybe Gidge has come back as Harris!*

I wanted to ask, but I was scared. What if I was wrong?

Would Harris be insulted if I accused him of being an old lady?

Would it be weird if I hugged him?

At least I knew the answer to *that* question. Yes. Because even if he turned out to be Gidge on the inside, he was still Harris on the outside — and I wasn't hugging Harris.

He wiped the tears off his face. He'd had almost stopped laughing by then, but he must have remembered what was so funny because he started up all over again. He threw back his head and slapped his knee.

Gidge used to do that too. If something was really funny, that's what she used to call it: a real knee-slapper.

Suddenly, Gidge coming back as Harris didn't seem so weird anymore. Why else would the letter say to bring him?

"Gidge?" I said.

Harris wheezed out, "Yes! " and I thought I'd finally found her but then he said, "Every time I think about her going over the side, it cracks me up." He slapped his knee again.

If Harris was Gidge, he clearly didn't know it.

Before I'd figured out what to do next, the roller coaster had made it to the top and was suddenly racing down the other side. Harris and I screamed. We screamed even louder when we went around a turn at the bottom and our heads went flying out to the side as if we were Labrador retrievers in an out-of-control pickup truck. Then the roller coaster slowed way, way down again until it almost stopped and then it began dragging its sorry old self up the next hill.

Harris had his hands over his face. "Man. That was *craaazy*," he said, which *really* reminded me of Gidge, and my heart went funny. But then he said, "I'm not sure I liked it," and I stopped thinking he was Gidge after all. She would have loved how scary it was.

The roller coaster kept climbing. I leaned over the edge and looked down on the amusement park grounds. I was hoping to see someone with a giant bunch of balloons or giving away free cotton candy or dancing to the rinky-dinky music coming out of the carousel — someone who I'd just know immediately was Gidge — but it was raining really hard now. The only people still at the park were standing under the awnings or running to get there.

"You see anyone who might be Gidge?" I said to Harris. Maybe I was missing something.

He looked over the side too. "No," he said, or I guess *moaned* is a better word. He lurched back up really quickly. His face was the color of an old tube sock. Kind of white, but mostly gray.

"Are you okay?"

"I don't like. Heights." It took him two swallows to get the sentence out.

"Why did you come on the roller coaster with me, then?"

"I didn't realize I didn't like them. Until now."

"Well, don't look over the side."

"I'm not." His head was flopped back on the seat, and he was looking straight up into the rain.

I could see his stomach suck in and bubble out. His chin jerked forward and his eyebrows went way up and I thought he was going to be sick in the little car with me.

"Close your eyes!" I said.

He did.

His stomach rippled in and out faster.

The car kept crawling up to the top. Harris made the kind of sounds a sad ghost would make.

"Think of something else," I said.

"All I can think of is how far up we are. And that I'm going to barf. And that it's going to get on your shoes if I do."

"They're rubber. That's okay." (I only said that to make him feel better. It's never okay to barf on someone's shoes.)

We got right to the very, very top of the highest hill. Then there was this weird grinding noise and the car stopped with a jerk and a bounce and a screech and a sigh.

"Don't worry. We'll be going back down soon. They'll probably stop the rides because of the weather." I wiped the water off my face with the back of my hand. "If you barf now, the rain will wash it away anyway."

Harris said, "Please don't say 'barf' again."

It was really pouring now. The guy down below put his hands around his mouth and hollered up, "Shouldn't be long, folks. Make yourself comfortable. We're just experiencing a few technical difficulties."

"Are we stuck?" Harris said.

"I think so."

"How high up are we?"

"Not very far."

He opened his eyes.

"But I wouldn't look if I were you," I said.

"Okay." He closed them again.

I patted his arm. I hung my head over the side and watched as, one by one, everybody left the park, and I knew I'd missed my chance to find Gidge.

We must have been stuck up there about an hour when Harris said, "I want to say something."

"Okay."

"I know you know what my dad did."

"No, I don't."

"Con didn't tell you?"

"No."

"Okay . . . But I bet you *imagined* what my dad did."

I didn't answer, but Harris was right. I imagined his dad doing all sorts of things. Robbing a bank, kidnapping a kid, burning down a rain forest. I knew it had to be something terrible if Harris wouldn't even admit he had a father.

Harris went, "I knew it."

"Sorry! What am I supposed to do? It's not like I can control my mind. If it was *my* father, you'd be imagining stuff too."

He thought about that for a second. "Yeah," he said. "I would."

"You don't have to tell me what he did if you don't want to," I said.

"No. I want to. I want to get it over with. It'll be easier telling you here when I don't have to look at you. Or, like, can't."

"True." Sometimes Pa and I would sit back to back when we had to say things we didn't want to say, like that time he admitted he ate all the KitKats from my Halloween bag. "I'm listening."

"My father got fired. He said it was because Carolyn — that's his boss — didn't like him so she gave his job to her boyfriend.

I thought that was unfair — so I hacked into the company's account. I sent all their email to a coffee shop in Kazakhstan and scrambled their files. I'm good at computers and they're not, so it was pretty easy. It took them ages to fix everything. I was really happy about it, until I found out Dad was lying."

"About what?"

Harris kind of laughed but not really. "Everything. He was depressed. He hadn't been doing his work for ages. When Carolyn found out she tried to help him, but he just got worse and worse and finally she had to let him go. Dad was too embarrassed to tell Mom, so he kept on pretending to go into the office. Then Mom found out because they had no money left in the bank. She was really upset so Dad made up this story about it all being Carolyn's fault. That's when I hacked into their accounts and the company found out it was me who messed things up and the police came and Mom found out Dad was lying and threw him out and now everyone's mad at me and that's why I can't use the internet anymore and why I'm living with Connie. Because of my dad."

It was really sad. I didn't know what to say, but the longer I didn't say anything the sadder it felt.

I patted his arm again. "I feel bad for you," I said.

"I feel bad for me too."

"But I also feel bad for your dad. He was depressed. He was sick. He couldn't help it."

"I know. But I'm still mad at him."

"Was it hard seeing him yesterday?"

"I don't know. More like weird. I get my hopes up that things are going to be better, that he's going to be Dad like he was before, but he isn't, and that just makes me feel worse. I'd rather not see him at all."

The wind blew and our car rattled. Harris groaned again. I moved my feet as far away from him as I could.

"I know how you feel," I said.

"You're trying not to barf too?"

"No. I mean about getting your hopes up. Every time I think I'm going to see Gidge I get excited and happy, but then it doesn't turn out. She comes into the shop but then she runs away with the green dress. She leaves me the ballerina but it's cheap and broken and doesn't mean anything. Then I think I figured out the clue in the letter, but we get here and all that happens is we end up stuck on the top of a roller coaster in the rain. It just makes me not want to hope any more. Not hoping would hurt way less than being disappointed all the time."

Harris was quiet for a while. Then he reached out to pat my arm, but since he couldn't open his eyes, he actually ended up patting my neck. That was okay. I knew what he meant.

"Maybe she *is* here," he said, "but we can't see her because she's in the air or the rain or something."

"Maybe. But what good is that? It's like smelling cookies come out of the oven and not being allowed to eat them. It's worse than not smelling them at all."

"Yeah. I get that."

I clunked my chin against the safety bar. "You think that's what Gidge meant by reincarnation? That she's just a spirit? That's all I can hope for?"

"I don't know. I got a book out of the library about reincarnation, but it was pretty confusing. Different people think different things. It sounds sort of like those build-your-own-teddy-bear places. You can pretty much make it whatever you want it to be."

"How come you got a book out of the library about it?"

"Not allowed to use the internet."

"No, I mean how come you wanted to learn about reincarnation?"

He shrugged. "I thought I should find out about it because of Gidge and you and whatever."

That was nice. I wanted to pat his arm again, but I didn't.

He talked a while about how the Hindus thought this and the Buddhists thought that and I sort of listened and sort of didn't, because Gidge didn't believe in organized religion so it didn't really matter what they thought. She was going to do reincarnation her way. I just didn't know what that was.

I said, "I'm never going to be happy again if Gidge doesn't come back. And not as some spirit. Not just some whiff I get off her clothes or some memory that pops into my head now and then. I'm not going to be happy until I can touch her and hold her and see her again. Not ever." I sucked in a big breath and held it there for a long time. "Sometimes I just want to go to The Pit of Despair and cry and cry and cry."

"The pit of despair? What's that?"

"Oh." I shook my head. I couldn't be bothered explaining. "Nothing. It's just what Gidge and I call our sad place."

Harris didn't say anything. I guess he understood about being sad so he just let me be for a while.

Then he said, "Yardley?"

"Yeah."

"You were the one who said Gidge would come back no matter what. Do you still believe that?"

"Yeah. I do." Or at least I wanted to. I'd never not believe Gidge.

"Then she'll turn up. Maybe not here. But somewhere. I mean, it's Gidge, right? You can count on her."

Half an hour later, the roller coaster started moving again and took us back to the bottom. Harris said, "Hallelujah," and we staggered off. His face was still pretty gray but at least he could open his eyes. We were wet and cold and hungry. We got on our scooters. He headed back to Over Easy. I went home.

I kept an eye out for Gidge the whole way.

CHAPTER

36

The next morning, I got up and put on my turquoise work boots, purple-striped leggings, denim shortie overalls and a white blouse with puffed sleeves and frilly cuffs that hung over my hands. I looked at myself in the mirror and laughed. Not because I didn't like my outfit, which I did, but because the blouse looked kind of pirate-y and that reminded me of Harris talking about pantaloons and how he knew I wanted them. He'd said it in a way that made me sound weird, but good-weird. I put in my Gidge barrette and got ready to go.

I told myself Harris was right about Gidge. She'd said she'd come back, so she'd come back. You don't stop believing in something just because it's hard to do. That's why Gidge always liked Martin Luther King and Anne of Green Gables and Mary Quant, who you probably don't know but she invented the miniskirt even though all the big fashion people were telling her it was "vulgar." Gidge liked people who kept believing even when the whole world told them they were wrong.

I got on my scooter and took off for Over Easy.

Along the way, there was a guy doing chalk portraits on the sidewalk. I stopped and watched him for a while because it's kind of hard not to, so I was a little late getting to the shop. I pushed open the door and the bell tinkled. It felt like a happy sound, like someone was trying to get your attention at a party or your kindergarten teacher was about to hand out snacks or a butterfly was going to come twinkle-toe-ing onto the stage in one of my parents' plays.

I wanted Harris to see my shirt.

"Ahoy, mateys!" I said, and slammed the door like a pirate.

"Why, ahoy yourself!" Con said. He was sitting on a stool at the counter sewing a fabric belt onto a pair of linen palazzo pants. "Don't you look swashbuckling this morning."

I put my hands on my hips as if I was Captain Hook and went, "You like?"

"I *love*. I'm all about a dramatic sleeve, and that's a beaut."

"Isn't it though?" I gave my arm a little jiggle. I waited for Harris to make some crack about it.

No sound. I looked around. I didn't see him.

"Where's Harris?"

Con had just put a couple of pins in his mouth, so he kept his teeth together when he answered. "Gone to the post office to get the mail."

"This early?"

"He was a little antsy this morning. Said he wanted to get out of here for a while."

I folded my scooter up and put it in the broom closet. "So he'd miss me, you mean?"

"No!" Con took the pins out of his mouth and stuck them in his little red tomato pincushion. He frowned. "Why would you say that?"

I shrugged.

"Something happen yesterday with you two?" he asked.

"Nothing bad."

"So why do you think he wouldn't want to see you, then?"

"He told me about his dad."

"Oh." Con nodded and held the palazzo pants up for a look. "So you think he's embarrassed now? Wishing he'd kept his mouth shut?"

"Yeah. I was even feeling a little embarrassed to see him this morning, thinking he'd be a little embarrassed to see me."

"Oh, the great circle of shame!" Con laughed. "Well, there's no doubt a bit of that. His father was in a difficult situation and maybe didn't handle it as well as he could have. Harris shouldn't feel embarrassed about it, but people are funny, aren't we? I was mortified when my friends found out my father didn't speak English very well."

I remembered Pa splopping into the props room in that

dumb bug outfit. That had embarrassed me. Why wouldn't Harris feel embarrassed about what his father did?

"Go figure, eh?" Con said. "Harris will be fine, though. He's among friends! To tell you the truth, I think he was actually looking forward to seeing you today. This was the first morning I didn't have to drag him out of bed when the alarm went off."

Con finished fixing the pants and gave them to me to steam-press. Harris came back from the post office about ten minutes later.

Con rubbed his hands together. "Anything interesting?"

Harris shrugged. "Didn't really look." He handed him a pile of mail all held together with a fat rubber band. Then he noticed me in the corner.

"Nice shirt," he said. "Did you forget your pantaloons?"

Con snickered. "Pantaloons." He had his head down and was flipping through the mail on the counter. "Look at you with the lingo, Harris. You're going to be a fashionista in no time . . . Oh, hey, Yard-ley!" He kind of sang out my name.

I'd been looking down ever since Harris said "pantaloons." I didn't know how hard I was supposed to laugh at his joke, so I didn't want anyone to see my face, but then I realized Con was waving another letter from Gidge and I didn't care anymore. I ran over and grabbed it.

"Thank you, thank you, thank you!"

"Don't thank me. I'm just the messenger."

I tore it open without even sniffing or *gazing upon* it. Red lipstick got all over my thumb and I almost ripped the card. I read it, moving my face from side to side just like they do in the cartoons.

Greetings, Earthling!
    I saw you yesterday on the roller coaster with your friend Harris.
I wanted to talk to you but you were stuck at the top and I was stuck at the bottom. I don't want that to happen again so I've come back for good. I'm here with you now.
    Love,
    Gidge

"Are you all right?" Con said. "Do you need to sit down?"
"No. No. I'm fine. Why?"
"You've gone winter-white. What did she say? Did she say something to upset you? Don't forget, she wrote these letters a long time ago. She didn't want you to be lonely. So she . . ."
"No. She said something good."
Harris said, "What?"
"She said she's here now." My face practically cracked in two from happiness.

Con had one of those lame smiles on his face, the kind adults put on when they think they're going to have to explain something to you in smaller words, but Harris went, "She is? Where?" He sounded as excited as I was.

"Gidge?" I went. "Gidge!" Harris and I raced around the store, checking in the dressing room, behind the counter, under the clothing racks as if the Karma Bunny had sent us on an egg hunt.

The place was empty. I went up to each of the mannequins and looked them right in the eyes and went, "Gidge? Is that you? Are you in there?" hoping they'd blink or laugh or throw their cold plastic arms around me. But nothing. For one horrible second, I had this feeling Gidge had come back as a beanie, or a choker, or a lace-up corset, and I was going to spend the rest of my life with a fashion accessory.

Con went, "Hey!" We turned and looked at him. "Did you leave the door open when you came in, sport?"

Harris went, "Oh, sorry," and pushed it closed.

"Too late!" Con said. "Look what snuck in." He leaned down behind the counter and picked up a cat. She was white and fat and very, very furry.

"Aren't you a pretty kitty? Yes you are. Yes you are." He held her against his shoulder and stroked her back. She purred. "Wow. Look at her gorgeous coat! Have you ever seen anything so thick? I wonder what kind she is."

Harris said, "A Norwegian forest cat." He went over and started to pet her, but I stayed back because I'm allergic to cats.

I looked at Harris and laughed. "How would you know that?" I'd always just thought a cat was a cat was a cat. Who knew there were different kinds?

He shrugged and blushed.

Con went, "You're asking how Harris knows something?! Because he's got a mind like a steel trap. That's why he's so good at puzzles. The kid remembers everything!"

The cat batted its paw against Con's head and we laughed. "Oh, sorry, Puss. Not getting enough attention, are you? We'd better get you back to your owner." He checked her collar for a tag but there wasn't one. "Now where are you from? What's your name?"

And that's when the cat turned her head and looked right at me with her big green eyes. I knew immediately who it was.

"Her name's Gidge," I said.

CHAPTER
37

"Oh, honey." Con pouted at me. "That's sweet. But this isn't our cat. We can't be giving her a new name. We'll do up flyers and put them on telephone poles. Her owner's bound to be missing her."

I took the cat out of his arms and held her close.

"No," I said. "This is Gidge. Like, *the* Gidge. She's come back. She's reincarnated."

"Honey . . ."

"Con, I know you don't believe me, but it's true. That letter I just got? That's what it said. 'I'm here with you now.' There was no one else in the store but us. Then this cat walked in? Who do you think it is?" I had to clear my throat.

"I think it's a cat, Yardley. A lost cat."

"A cat, yes. But not lost." I rubbed my nose with the back of my hand. "She's not lost at all. She's found. This is Gidge . . ." I sneezed. "Back with me . . . just like she promised. We're finally . . ." I sneezed four times, and each time my head bounced up and down like I was banging it off a table. I wiped my face in my elbow. "Together."

"Yardley. Why don't you give her to me?" Con put his arms out to take the cat.

I stepped away from him, shaking my head. "No. I'm . . . I'm . . . I'm . . ." — another sneeze — "never letting her go again."

"But, sweetie, you're obviously allergic to her, and I honestly don't think Gidge would come back as something you're allergic too, now, would she?"

"Well, she did!"

Con gave a closed-mouth smile with frowny eyes.

"Harris!" I said. "Help me out here." I rubbed my eye. My left one was super itchy. "This is Gidge, right? I mean, look at her!"

My mouth opened really wide as if a dentist was pulling out my molars, and my neck bent back and my body froze while a giant sneeze worked its way up from the bottom of my stomach and exploded out of my face.

"Harris?" I said when I'd caught my breath again. "Tell him. This is Gidge, right?"

"Um."

"Harris."

"Well, she did say she'd come back, and her fur is kind of like Gidge's hair."

"And her eyes?" I said, turning her around so he could get a better look.

"They're, um," he leaned forward and squinted, "they're green."

"Exactly! Like Gidge's."

"Yeah, but . . . ," Harris said, and I knew he was deserting me too.

"But what? This is Gidge." I started coughing really hard. "It's Gidge. I can tell. She's come back."

Harris reached out his arms. "I can hold her if you want to wipe your nose."

I handed him Gidge, but only because the snot was starting to tickle the top of my lips and I was worried it was going to get in my mouth.

Con gave me his hankie. I sneezed into it for quite a while. When I opened my eyes, I saw Con whispering to Harris.

When he caught me looking, he said, "You okay, honey?"

"I'm fine. Not like I haven't had allergies before."

"Are you worse this time? Because if you are, that's a bad sign."

"No," I said. But I was. I'd never sneezed this hard in my life.

Con looked at me for a while. I tried not to scratch my eyes.

"I'm taking you home," he said. "You need to have a shower and wash the cat hair off you, then you need to take an antihistamine to clear out your system. Harris, can you stay here and hold the fort while I drive Yardley home?"

"Yeah, sure, okay."

I reached out to take Gidge from him.

Con gently pushed my hands down. "I think she'd better stay here while you get cleaned up. Harris will look after her, won't you, bud?"

"Yeah, I'll get her some milk."

"Soy," I said, because that's what Gidge liked.

Con put his arm around me and led me to his car. "She'll be fine with Harris. He's always liked animals," he said. "And Gidge."

He opened the door for me, and I got in the front seat. Harris was standing in the window watching. He raised Gidge's paw and waved it at me. Con backed out. We hadn't even gone a block when I realized I'd forgotten my backpack. I told him to stop.

"I can't stop here," he said. There was a lot of traffic that day. "You sure you need it?"

"It's got my house keys in it."

"Okay. You run in and get it. I'll drive around the block."

That's all I was going to do — get my backpack — because by then I did feel pretty bad. But when I went into the shop, I noticed Harris and Gidge the Cat weren't there. And then I remembered Con whispering to Harris. Had Con told him to get rid of the cat while he took me home? Were they in this together? Harris had pulled me away from the lady in the pink suit. Maybe he was trying to keep me away from Gidge again.

I heard something coming from Con's office. A slow tap, tap, tap and then a whoosh sound. It sounded familiar but I didn't know why at first.

I tiptoed to the office and peeked my head in the door.

Harris was sitting at Con's desk with his back to me. The cat was curled up by his feet. One of Gidge's squished Kleenex cards was lying on the desk, half open. The matching envelope was in the typewriter and Harris was typing an address onto it with two fingers. He finished, pulled the envelope out of the roller and slipped the card inside.

My body didn't move but my brain was racing around like crazy, picking up words and memories and weird things that never quite made sense and turning them this way and that way until they all fit together.

It was Harris, I realized.

Harris had sent me the notes. Made everything up and signed Gidge's name at the bottom. He must have seen Gidge typing up letters after her chemo sessions. He must have known she'd left some extra cards in Con's office. He must have wanted to ruin my life.

"You tricked me!" I screamed.

Harris jumped so high that the cat squealed and Con's wheely chair spun around. Harris's eyes were open really wide and his face was really pale, and he was wearing bright red lipstick.

The puzzle pieces in my brain moved again. I saw the lipstick. I noticed the envelope in his hand. He was even going to seal it with a kiss! Somehow that made me even madder.

"*You* wrote the letters?"

"No." He put his hands up in front of him like he was worried I was going to hit him or something. (He obviously knew what I was thinking.)

"Yes, you did!"

"No. I didn't. I mean, not all of them. Just the last two. The first one was from Gidge. For true, Yardley. I . . . I . . ."

"You made up the thing about the cat?"

He squeezed his eyes together and nodded.

"Why would you do that?"

"Because . . . because you said you wouldn't be happy until you had Gidge to hold again. So I bought a cat —"

"You *bought* me a cat?!" Why was everyone always doing this to me? Pawning off any old piece of junk on me as if I was too stupid to notice it wasn't the real thing. Milo hadn't been a real friend, Harris wasn't either, and that dumb cat sure as hell wasn't Gidge. "Why? How did you even get a cat?!?"

"Craigslist. I took the money from the cash register. Don't tell Con. Please. I'll pay him back. I was just trying to —"

"Why would you do that? Why did you trick me?"

"I wasn't doing it to trick you! I was doing it to save you."

"Save me? *You* save *me*? From what?"

"From getting hurt."

"*You're* the one hurting me. You keep doing this to me! You're the one who pulled me away from the lady. You're the one who —"

"That lady didn't want you, Yardley. That's why I —"

"How do you know? You think you're so smart just because you can do puzzles, but you aren't!"

"I know. I know I'm not. But I saw her face and her pushing you away, and I don't know much about reincarnation but I was sure if that was Gidge she wouldn't be mean to you like that."

"Yeah, well, I saw her face too, and I saw Gidge. That was the *only* time I saw Gidge! That was the only chance I had to find her, and you ruined it!" I was really screaming at him now because I was so mad, and sometimes the only thing you can do is scream at a person, especially if they say something terrible that you can't help thinking is true.

"And I went to see her, too," Harris said. Quietly now, which just made it worse.

"What?" I'd stopped screaming but my heart hadn't realized it yet.

"The lady. After Con got mad at me for fighting with you that time. I left the store. I went to see her. I wanted to know who she was and how she knew about Gidge and the green velvet dress. But she wouldn't tell me anything." He wiped the lipstick off with his thumb. "Anything . . . except that she doesn't want to see you, Yardley. She doesn't want to have anything to do with you or Gidge. She said so."

"Shut up," I said.

I could hear Con honking outside.

"Shut up," I said again, "and give me her address."

"I . . . I don't remember it."

"You do so. You've got a mind like a steel trap. That's what Con said, and he's right. You never forget anything."

Con honked some more. It was a busy street so he couldn't stop for long without other drivers getting mad. After a while, the honking stopped. He must have headed off around the block again.

I pushed out my jaw and squinted my eyes at Harris and said it again. "Where does she live?"

"I don't know."

"Yes, you do. You went to see her. What was the address?"

He didn't say anything.

"This is what you do, Harris. You meddle in other people's lives. Remember what happened last time you butted your stupid face into someone else's life? You messed it up big time. Don't mess up mine."

That was mean, but it worked. He gave me her address.

I didn't even thank him. Why should I? I grabbed my backpack and scooter out of the hall closet. I checked to make sure Con was nowhere around, then I headed to 1131 Hart Lane.

CHAPTER 38

Hart Lane was a little street just at the edge of the city. Big trees hung over the pavement and blocked out most of the sun, so the only light getting through looked like giant sequins sparkling in the leaves. I smiled. It was like hope was puffing up my lungs.

I scootered down the street until I found number 1131. It was the type of house kids draw. White with black trim and windows with a cross in the middle. The door was turquoise. The garden out front was full of flowers. The path up to the door was curved and made of flat stones with moss growing up between them. I took off my helmet and patted my head to make sure my piece of Gidge was still in my hair. I smoothed my blouse and pulled up my knee socks. I wanted to look my best.

"Wish me luck," I said to the universe, then I rang the doorbell.

CHAPTER 39

There was no answer, so I rang the bell again. A couple of seconds later, I heard footsteps coming downstairs. They stopped at the door.

"Hello?" I said.

There was a little round peephole in the door, about the size of a dime. I was pretty sure I saw something move behind it.

"Mrs. Johnson?" I could tell she was there. "I'm Yardley."

Silence.

"Gidge's granddaughter."

"I know who you are."

"I'd like to talk to you."

"Well, I don't want to talk to you. Or to Gidge, if that's why you're here. I didn't open her letters. I sent them back. I got another one today and I'm going to send that one back too. I thought I made it very clear I wanted nothing to do with her, but I guess she's gotten dense in her old age. So why don't you go back and tell her to just leave me alone?"

Every word she said felt like rocks hitting me in the head. That's how much they hurt.

"I don't think I can," I said.

She laughed the way you do when you want to make someone feel bad. "She won't listen to you either, eh? Ha! She's always been stubborn. A real mule. You can tell her I said that, too."

"No, I can't."

"Oh yeah? How come?"

"Because she's dead." And for the first time I realized that was true. Gidge was dead. Really dead. Gone.

Mrs. Johnson didn't say anything for quite a long time, and then she went, "What?" in a little voice.

"She's dead. She died. And you wouldn't read her letters. And I don't know why except maybe you're mean. And you made her sad. And she tried. I don't know what she wanted to say to you, but I know it wouldn't have been mean." I wanted to say more but the words *she's dead* just kept screaming in my head. My bottom lip went crazy and I knew I wouldn't be able to get the words out if I even had any, which I didn't, so I took off on my scooter and I didn't stop, not once, not even after I'd gone miles and miles and miles.

Gidge was dead, so what difference did anything make? I was dead too. That's how I felt. I was going to go where no one would ever find me.

CHAPTER
40

The Pit of Despair was really far away. You went on a paved road until you got to an old-fashioned diner with a giant smiling hotdog in its parking lot. A little ways past that, there was a speed limit sign, and if you looked through the trees you could see a brook. You crossed the brook and went through the woods and after a while you'd come to a path and the path would take you to an old dirt road and the old dirt road would take you to The Pit. That's all I remembered about how to find it. I'd never gone there on my own before. I'd always gone with Gidge.

I found the diner after a few tries. A lady inside let me use her phone so I called Con and apologized for running off. I told him I went home on my scooter. He was probably mad, but he said, "That's okay, honey. As long as you're fine." I said I was. I'd pretty much stopped sneezing since he'd made me give the cat to Harris, so I wasn't lying, at least about that.

I got back on my scooter and found the speed limit sign with a brook beside it. We'd had a lot of rain lately so the brook was way bigger than before. My shoes got soaked when I tried to jump the rocks and then I fell and my pirate shirt got soaked too because I dropped my scooter and had to lean in to get it. The path was pretty overgrown so I got lost for a while, but then I remembered there were deserted railway tracks that went right there and I found them and followed them for a while until I came to a clearing and there was The Pit.

I actually smiled. The Pit reminded me of Gidge and how happy I used to be when I was with her, even if we only went there when we were sad. It was just like she'd said in her letter — the beauty and the bumps — which made me smile some more because Gidge was always right about stuff like that. Then it hit me again that she was dead and it was just me now, which meant just bumps, and I was pretty sure that was what my life was going to be from now on. Bump, bump, bump, bump. Like falling down the stairs and ending in a little broken pile of bones at the bottom.

I didn't even cry when I thought that because what was the point? It was just the truth.

I suddenly realized how tired I was. The old jelly bean camper-trailer was still standing beside The Pit. It wasn't fancy but I could lie down there. It would be okay. I could stay there. Maybe forever. I remembered Gidge and me picking blueberries around there once. I wouldn't starve. And even if I did, I wouldn't care.

The door to the camper had come off its hinges and one of the wheels was flat so everything was tilted. It was tiny inside. There was a little table about the size of a cafeteria tray attached to the wall and a little bench with a padded cushion under the back window. The green leatherette of the cushion was all torn up and white stuffing was coming out like fake smoke from a gingerbread house. The cupboard doors were hanging open and the cupboards were empty except for a couple of mugs and a pot without a handle and a large jar of coffee creamer that had turned hard as rock. The floor was covered with pinecones and leaves and other stuff that falls off trees. I was pretty sure someone or something had peed inside the place, too. It didn't smell very good. I sat in the doorway with my feet on the steps and looked out at the big gray cliffs of The Pit. Gidge used to write on them. She liked to get bad things out of her system and move on.

I wished I had some chalk but then I thought, "Why?" In the whole world, there was not enough chalk for me to write all the bad stuff I was feeling.

"Gidge," I said, because there was nothing else to say.

After a while I realized the sky was getting darker. I was wet and hungry and too tired to go searching for blueberries.

I looked in my backpack and found two cold, squished cork-screw fries that I'd forgotten to give the pigeons. They were really old and linty but I ate them anyway. Then I started getting cold, too. I knew I should go home, but why would I? Gidge wouldn't be there, Pa and Mima would probably send me to camp, and I didn't have any friends.

Which made me think of Harris. He wasn't my friend. He just got stuck with me, the same way I got stuck with him, and then he butted his nose into my business and made everything worse.

I rummaged around in my backpack for more French fries but all I found was the broken ballerina. I took her out. Her arm fell off. I remembered the lady from the antique store saying there used to be two dancers holding hands. One without the other was worth nothing. That was exactly how I felt. Gidge was gone, and now I was worth nothing.

I picked up a pinecone and threw it out of the trailer, just for something to do. I kept throwing pinecones until it got dark. Nobody came, not even a bird or a squirrel. I crawled inside the camper and lay down on the floor. I lay on my side with my head on my backpack and my hands between my knees. I put the ballerina beside me. I was cold and the stuff on the floor hurt my ribs. I wanted to go to sleep so I wouldn't have to think any more. I closed my eyes, but I kept thinking and thinking and thinking and thinking and none of it was good, but I couldn't stop.

I wanted to die. That's all I wanted to do but I didn't.

I fell asleep.

When I woke up, Gidge was leaning over me.

CHAPTER
41

"Yardley." She shook me. "Is that your name? Yardley? Say something."

The moon was coming in through the open door behind her. It didn't give off much light, but it lit up her hair — her beautiful wild white hair — so I knew it was her.

"Gidge!" I threw my arms around her. I nuzzled my face into her neck. I breathed in as hard as I could and inhaled her cloud. I let myself feel happy for five seconds, then I pulled away.

"You're not Gidge, are you?"

She shook her head. "No. I'm Margaret. Margaret Johnson."

I sat back on my heels. "Mrs. Johnson." I'd actually hugged mean Mrs. Johnson.

"Afraid so. Are you okay?" She sounded worried.

"Um. Yeah." More than anything, I was confused. I said, "What did you do to your hair? Why did you make it look like Gidge's?"

She reached up and touched it. "It's what I *didn't* do to my hair. I didn't straighten it. I've been too upset to even get myself properly dressed, ever since I spoke with that boy."

"Harris?"

"I don't know what his name is. The one who told me you were Gidge's granddaughter. He came to my house after I'd been at the shop that day. I told him to get out, go away. It was just so upsetting hearing Gidge's name again. Thinking that someone I'd once been so close to had a family I knew nothing about! I completely fell apart. Didn't shower. Didn't put my makeup on. Didn't do my hair. Gidge always let hers go wild but I've straightened mine every day of my life since we were teenagers."

"You knew Gidge since you were teenagers?"

"Longer. Since we were babies. Gidge and I were sisters . . ."

"What?" My insides froze.

"I'm your Great-Aunt Madge."

"No." I shook my head. Gidge would have told me. We told each other everything. "Gidge didn't have a sister."

"She did, I'm afraid. I'm not a very good one, but I *am* her sister."

"I don't believe you."

"Let me see if I can convince you, then." She rummaged around in her purse and took out her phone. "How do you turn on the flashlight on this thing?"

I showed her. She took off her glasses and shone the

flashlight on herself. "Doesn't this face look a little familiar to you?"

Her nose was a bit longer than Gidge's and her mouth was a bit smaller and she didn't have as many laugh-lines around her eyes, but I could definitely see the resemblance.

"People used to think we were twins. There's only a year between us," she said. "Bridget and Margaret. Gidge and Madge. That's what our mother called us. It's been a long time since I last saw her, but I can't believe we would have changed that much." She brought her hand up to her forehead and wiped her hair away. Her face may have been a little different, but that was Gidge's hand. Even I could see that.

"Why didn't she tell me about you?"

"Probably the same reason I didn't tell my own kids about Gidge. I was ashamed."

"Of what?"

"Of having been so stupid."

I waited for her to tell me more, but she just said, "Are you cold?"

I'd kind of forgotten about my body. "A little."

She snuggled up next to me and wrapped a blanket around us. "The Pit has always been cold at night, so I brought supplies."

It was only then I realized how weird it was that she was even here.

"How did you know where I was?"

"I didn't."

"So why did you come?"

"This is where Gidge and I came when we were kids. We used to live nearby. It was the country back then. We found it when we were exploring. The gravel pit had been closed for years. Gidge was the one who named it The Pit of Despair. We'd been reading *Anne of Green Gables* at the time. That's the type of name Anne would have given it."

"Funny we never ran into you here," I said. Gidge and I went to The Pit quite a few times.

"Not really. I moved away when I got married. I was gone for thirty-five years. I moved back when I got divorced but I only came to The Pit once after that."

"How come?"

"I saw chalk-writing on the rocks. I knew Gidge had been there. I didn't want to bump into her, so I never came back. Until now."

Avoiding Gidge. Wanting *not* to be near her. My brain could not compute. "Why did you hate her so much?"

"Hate her?" She turned and looked at me in surprise. "I didn't hate Gidge!"

"Sure sounds like you did."

"No. I hated *us*, I guess, what we'd become."

"I don't understand."

She gave a big, long sigh and shook her head. Her hair wobbled just like Gidge's used to. It always made me think of an underwater sea creature.

"How can I explain something like this?" she said. "It all just sounds so ridiculous."

"I'm okay with ridiculous."

"Well, you asked for it then . . . " She gave a sad laugh. "Gidge and I looked a lot alike, but we were very different people. The way our minds worked, and I guess our hearts, too. It wasn't a problem until our mother died. Up until then, we were best friends. But losing Mum when we were teenagers made us both really sad. Gidge's way of being sad was to show it. Mine was to hide it. It hurt me to talk about my feelings. It hurt Gidge *not* to talk about hers. The more she needed from me, the more I needed to get away from her. We ended up being mad at each other all the time, instead of being sad together. Dad couldn't help because he was grieving, too. Worse, he was like me. He didn't want to talk about it either. Dad hid out in his work shed and I hid out in the library. We both wanted to get away from Gidge and her big, loud, messy feelings. I thought she was hysterical. She thought I was uptight. So we grew apart. The truth was we were both just really sad."

"Yeah," I said. I knew what that was like.

She squeezed my hand.

"Anyway . . . We had a fight, one of many, but somehow this was the one that stuck."

"What happened?"

"I'm almost embarrassed to tell you." She rolled her eyes. "We were in our late teens. That's how long ago it was! We didn't have much money and we were the same size so we shared clothes. We both wanted a new dress so we made a deal. I'd pay for the fabric and Gidge would sew it. She was always better at that sort of thing than I was — plus, even then, she had a real eye for design.

"There was a party one night that we both wanted to go to. Gidge had finished the dress and it looked gorgeous. I thought I should wear it because I paid for it. She thought she should wear it because she did all the work. We got into a big fight. She called me a name, said I was greedy. I called her another name and threw our music box at her. Dad came storming up from downstairs, saw the box broken in a million pieces and got furious. Our mother had given it to us. It was one of the few things we had left from her."

"Is that where this is from?" I picked the broken ballerina up off the floor beside me.

Mrs. Johnson turned the flashlight on it. "Where did you get that?"

"It was in the parcel with the green velvet dress. It must have fallen out when . . . when I grabbed you at the shop.

Harris found it. Then I found a note from Gidge saying something like 'We were meant to be together just like these ballerinas.' I thought she was talking about me and her, but I guess . . . I guess she was talking about you."

"Oh, dear . . . So true. I see that now." Mrs. Johnson sucked in a little jittery breath. "We were."

She put her arm around me and leaned her head against mine. She touched the ballerina with the tip of her finger. "When we were little, we'd pretend the dancers were us. This one was supposed to be me. See her tiara? My tiara had a green jewel. Gidge's had a blue one."

She picked up the corner of the blanket and dabbed her nose. "Nobody could put us back together again either. That stupid fight. We could just never let it go."

"That's sad."

"It is. We should have patched things up when we had the chance but we'd moved too far apart. Gidge got into all that hippie stuff and I did the corporate thing. We both thought the other person was a bit crazy. I married and moved away. Our father died. There was no reason to get in touch after that, and I'd have been too proud to, in any case." She shook her head. "And all because of a dress. Gidge wore it to the party, but after that neither of us ever put it on again. Can you believe it?"

I remembered something. "When I asked Gidge why she didn't like the dress, she said it didn't bring out the best in her.

I thought she meant it made her legs look short or her bum look flat or something, but I guess she meant something different."

"Ha. It didn't bring out the best in me, either. You ever hear about those people who take a little thing and build it up into something fabulous? Well, the truth is you can take a little thing and build it up into something terrible, too. And you know what the worst part of all this is? I can't even remember for sure if I was the one who threw the music box and that's why I got grounded, or if Gidge threw the music box and I got grounded because Dad heard me swear. In any event, that was the straw that broke the camel's back and we were both just too stubborn to do anything about it."

"Gidge was pretty stubborn — but I never thought she was *that* bad."

"Well, at least when she realized how ridiculous the whole thing was she got stubborn about trying to make it right. More than you can say about me! She'd been sending me letters for ages, but I just kept sending them back unopened. I always thought I'd get around to making up with her. Like in those TV sitcoms where everybody ends up hugging right before the music comes on at the end, but I left it too late. Maybe if I'd read her letters and found out she was dying . . . but I didn't. She had to trick me into coming into your store with that stupid contest."

That was when it hit me. "You're The Free Gift Queen!"

"I am. At least that's what they called me in that newspaper article. Me and my contests. I would have said, 'what a waste of time' except now I know that's how Gidge found me . . . That's what she said in her letter."

"What letter? I thought you didn't read them."

"I didn't — except for the one I got today. After you left . . . after you told me she was dead, I was finally brave enough to read what she had to say."

"And . . ."

"She said she hoped I'd fallen for her trick and gone to Over Easy. She thought all I'd have to do was see you even once and that would be enough to end this silly feud. She thought you and I could help each other. That we'd like each other. I'm afraid that so far I haven't given you much to like, but if you're willing to forgive an old —"

The flashlight on her phone died and everything suddenly went pitch-black. We both screamed.

"Oh, dear," Mrs. Johnson said, when she'd caught her breath again. "Should have charged this damn thing. Didn't realize I'd be needing it. Do you have one?"

"Nope." We only have one cellphone in our family and my parents need it.

"I guess we're here until morning, then. Good thing we're together."

"Yeah," I said. And it was.

CHAPTER 42

This is Harris. Yardley missed what happened next so I'm going to tell you that part. I'll also straighten out a couple things she got wrong. (I'm not saying Yardley was lying. I'm just saying she didn't know what really happened.)

That day when she caught me writing the letters? Yardley was so mad. She took off as soon as she got Mrs. Johnson's address out of me. Con came into the shop a few minutes later. He asked where she was. I said I didn't know. I said I thought she'd got in the car with him.

I shouldn't have lied, but I didn't want to snitch on Yardley, especially since it was my fault she ran away. I shouldn't have tricked her into believing Gidge was writing to her. It only made everything worse. I also lied to Con, because I knew he'd be mad at me for meddling again. Yardley was right. That's what got me into trouble in the first place.

But what could I do? Yardley thought I was doing it just to mess up her life, but that's not true. I did it because I was worried about her. I remembered when Dad found out I hacked the company email. You should have seen the look on his face. It wasn't even mad or furious or any of those things. It was like this whole new word that means something like *I'm angry and disappointed and ashamed and I don't ever want to see you again* all rolled into one. I was afraid Mrs. Johnson was going to give Yardley a face like that too. Once you've seen someone look at you like that, you never forget it.

Plus — and this is the big reason I stuck my nose in — I got a letter from Gidge. A real letter. Sealed with a kiss and everything.

I always liked Gidge when she was alive. She was the only one who looked at me and didn't see everything I did wrong. (Even Con did that. He loves me and everything, but I could tell he kept hoping I'd change. Finally start doing things right.) So I was happy to get her letter. I waited until I could read it in private. She said a lot of stuff in it that I'm not going to tell you because it was just for me, but she also said that I shouldn't feel bad about hacking those email accounts. She wouldn't want me to do it again, but she said it showed I was a helper, and that was a good thing because the world needs more people who will step in and help even when they're afraid to.

Gidge said Yardley was going to be lonely and scared for a while. She thought I might know something about how that feels so she asked me to help her get through it.

That was all I was trying to do. Help Yardley. That's why I went to Mrs. Johnson's. That's why I wrote the letters. That's why I got that dumb cat. And that's why I didn't tell Con that Yardley had gone to find Mrs. Johnson.

I was really happy when Yardley called the shop a little while later and told Con she was home. She said she was sorry that she'd made him wait. Con said, "That's okay, honey. As long as you're fine." Then he hung up and turned to me and said, "Poor kid. She's not herself. She misses Gidge."

And I smiled, which must have looked weird, but that was because I thought she'd decided not to go to Mrs. Johnson's. I had no idea what Gidge did to the lady, but it couldn't have been good. It seemed weird to think Gidge would have stolen her dress, but how would I know? I didn't think my dad would ever lie about stuff either, but he did, and I mean like *big time*. Adults can be just as bad as kids when you think about it.

I wasn't worried about Yardley until Con and I were playing a video game that night and his phone rang and it was her parents going, "Where is she? Where'd she go? She never does this," etc., etc.

Then Con hung up and was like, "All right. What's going on here?" and he was so mad and scared that I told him the truth. About the ballerina and the letters and Mrs. Johnson.

Things went crazy after that. Con called Yardley's parents back. They called the police. The police put out an emergency bulletin saying there was a missing child and I gave them Mrs. Johnson's address. They went to her house and they knocked and knocked and knocked but there was no answer so they kicked down the door. Nobody was home and her car was gone so the police came back to our place. They kept asking me if I thought Mrs. Johnson had abducted Yardley and I said I didn't know because, like, seriously . . . how do you know what another person's going to do?

Yardley's parents were there too. People sat in chairs with their hands folded between their knees and talked in really calm voices. They didn't want to upset me. They just wanted me to think. Had Yardley said anything to me about where she was going? I said she wouldn't have told me because she was really mad at me and didn't like me. Con patted my shoulder and said she didn't mean those things. Yardley wasn't in a good frame of mind. And I said, "Yeah, I know, sometimes she just wanted to go to the pit of despair and cry," because that's what she told me on the roller coaster.

And her dad said, "What did you say?"

So I went, "She wants to cry in the pit of despair."

And he went, "The Pit of Despair? She said that?" and I said yeah.

And her dad jumped up and said, "That's where she is!"

And then all the adults were going, "What? Where? Huh? The pit of what?" and that was the first time I realized it was a real place and not just a feeling Yardley had.

"Gidge went there when she was upset," Yardley's dad said. He wasn't dressed in his bug costume but he still had some makeup on so his eyes looked kind of weird.

The cops asked where it was, but he put his hands on his hips and made a face and shook his head. "I went there a few times with my mother but that was when I was a kid. It's just an old gravel pit. Nobody uses it anymore." And one of the cops went, "The old Kearney Brothers quarry?" And Yardley's dad shrugged, and then they looked at me like I should know but I shrugged too, and the older cop said, "That's the only gravel pit I've ever heard of around here and I've been on the job thirty-two years," so they all decided that must be it and everyone got ready to go.

Before they left, that cop shook my hand and said, "You've been a big help, son," and Con put his arm around my shoulder and said, "He has." Nobody mentioned that I was the reason Yardley ran away in the first place.

She can tell you the rest from here.

CHAPTER
43

heard a dog barking, but it sounded far away.

I felt like I was under the ocean or on a mountain or in space and I needed to swim or climb or fly to get back to the world. I knew that was impossible, or maybe I just wanted it to be, so I tried not to hear the dog, but it kept barking and barking and barking, and then someone was calling my name, too, and I knew I had to get up.

I opened my eyes. It wasn't *dark* dark anymore, just sort of dark, but it still took me a second to realize where I was and that the person sleeping next to me wasn't Gidge.

More voices were calling, "Yardley!" and I could tell that one of them was Mima's and another was Pa's, so I went, "I'm here! I'm here!" and that woke Mrs. Johnson up, and I remembered again that she was Gidge's sister because barking dogs wouldn't have woken Gidge up either since her hearing started getting bad.

She sat up with her hand on her heart and her face all confused, and I said, "It's okay, Mrs. Johnson. It's me. Yardley. We're at The Pit. They found us." And it took her a while, but she started to nod, and then laugh a little, and I took her arm and helped her up.

We stepped out of the jelly bean camper-trailer just as the cops and the dogs and my parents were getting there.

Dad took one look at Mrs. Johnson and went, "Gidge?" then passed out on the ground as if he'd just got an arrow right through the heart.

CHAPTER 44

Things happened pretty fast after that.

Mrs. Johnson and I ran out of the camper-trailer. Pa came to, and Mima had to explain what happened but I'm not sure he got it all. As soon as he saw me, he went kind of crazy, and Mima did too. They were like toddlers who'd got lost in the mall or something. Sobbing and howling and refusing to let go of me. I was just cold and hungry and sore and kind of happy knowing I could go home with them and they wouldn't be mad or make me go to camp.

The police took Mrs. Johnson and me to the hospital and gave us doughnuts to eat on the way. The doctors checked our temperatures and our hearts and everything and said we were okay to leave. It had been an unseasonably cold night, they said, and Mrs. Johnson had diabetes so her circulation wasn't too good, so it was lucky I'd been there to keep her warm.

Pa asked Madge — that's what she wanted us to call her — if she'd like to come to our place for breakfast.

She said, "Thank you very much, but I really couldn't." I told her she had to. She said I sounded just like Gidge — by which she meant *bossy* — but that she'd be happy to come. She'd wasted enough time already. She needed to get to know us before she was "past her best-before date." (She actually said that, which made me really and truly believe she was Gidge's sister.)

CHAPTER

45

When the medical school was through with Gidge's body, they gave us what was left and we had it cremated. We put her ashes in Pa's poo vase. We were going to throw them off the roller coaster but we decided against it because a) it's illegal to sprinkle corpse crumbs somewhere they could land on people and b) we thought of a better place.

The Pit of Despair. It was so perfect I didn't know why we hadn't thought of it before.

Everybody came. Pa and Mima and Con and Harris and Madge. I wanted Con and Harris to bring Gidge the Cat, too, but my parents didn't want me getting allergic so they left her at home. (She's Harris's cat now, and she's not like Gidge at all. She's a picky eater and she doesn't like people and she hisses whenever anyone puts on the Rolling Stones.)

We packed a big picnic and brought champagne. We all put on our best clothes. Con wore a fabulous sharkskin suit with skinny lapels and stovepipe trousers that he'd bought at an auction. He'd been planning to sell it in his new menswear section but he liked it so much he decided to keep it. Harris wore brand-new cargo shorts, which aren't my idea of high fashion but certainly fit his image. (Gidge was all about "you being you.") Madge wore a dress Gidge had designed for her Now or Neverland collection. Madge got a seamstress to make it out of purple paisley. It looked fierce on her. Pa and Mima wore their costumes from "A Smidgen of Gidge."

I wore the green velvet dress. Madge had it shortened and taken in at the sides, so you barely noticed I don't have boobs. I wore my Gidge barrette in my hair and all the bangles I could find on my arm and army boots on my feet. (It was a long walk into The Pit so I needed good hiking shoes, but I also just liked the way they looked with the dress.)

We gathered at the edge of The Pit and Pa asked us all to take a minute of silence to think about what Gidge meant to us. I closed my eyes and smiled. A minute wasn't long enough, but it didn't matter. I was always thinking about her.

When the time was up, Pa went, "Would you like to do the honors, YaYa?" and handed me the poo vase.

I threw the ashes into The Pit and thought, *The beauty and the bumps. The good and the bad. The laughter and the tears.* Gidge was all those things, and they were perfect.

Just then, out of nowhere, a breeze blew up, and suddenly the ashes were all coming right back at us. Everybody ducked and screamed and covered their eyes. When we stood up again, we were all covered in sparkles.

Gidge-sparkles. We bent over and tried to shake them off and tried to wipe them off but they clung to our hair and stuck to our clothes.

"I guess she's here to stay," Pa said, and we laughed and he poured the champagne.

That was a few months ago. It's hard to believe Gidge has been gone for so long. I'd like to say that having Great-Aunt Madge in my life is as good as having Gidge, but it isn't. She doesn't like to sew, she doesn't like to dance, and she has a thing for pastel colors that isn't going away any time soon, no matter how many times I say I'd like to see her in more jewel tones. But she laughs like Gidge and she's as stubborn as Gidge and she tells me stuff about Gidge that I never knew, so I always like talking to her.

One other way she's not like Gidge is that she's good at business. Madge had a company before she retired. She's talking about starting another one to produce Gidge's Now Or Neverland designs. She's also helping Pa and Mima run the Hoof & Mouth Theater. Since she got involved, the seats are full most nights and we have a real concession stand and even some sponsors. For the first time ever, no one seems too worried about money. We actually had enough this month to get a new (okay, *almost* new) fridge. Every time I get myself a nice cold glass of milk, I think of Gidge. She always talked about how the universe would look after us, but I think she gave the universe too much credit. It was Gidge who tricked Madge back into our lives. That was the secret Number Four Thing on her To-Die list. Bring us all together. We're all glad she did.

Harris and I are friends now too. Real friends. I gave him Gidge's scooter so we can go for rides together. Sometimes I help him with his puzzles, even if he doesn't really need my help. Sometimes we argue, and we still bug each other now and again, but we have fun. He's not quite my KooKoo, but I like him.

Gidge's cloud is gone but I know she's still with me. Metaphorically speaking. That's not as good as the real thing, but I'll take it.

CHAPTER
46

got one last letter from Gidge. It arrived on my thirteenth birthday.

Darling YaYa - - -
   I don't know where I'll be by the time you get this, but I do know, wherever I am, I'll be missing you. I'm sure you'll be missing me too, but I have faith in the universe - - - and, of course, in your utter fabulousness - - - so I know you'll find someone to take my place.
   That someone may be named Madge, and if so, it's proof that all our time on karma patrol paid off. She's strong and she's funny and, unlike

me, she's got an amazing head on her
shoulders. (My amazing head was
always floating off in the clouds.)
I dream of you becoming the best of
friends.

If Madge does take my place,
shower her with love and affection,
but do save a little for me in case
I ever pop by for a visit.

Until then, stay wild, Moon Child.
Your ever-loving Gidge
XOXOXOXOXOXOXO
P.S. I'll write again soon.

ACKNOWLEDGMENTS

Thanks to my astute and gracious editor Lynne Missen. Her suggestions are always so smart, constructive and delicately offered that I barely ever sulk. If this editing thing doesn't pan out, she'd make a great life coach.

Thanks to my forthright and dedicated agent Fiona Kenshole. I'm lucky to have her in my corner. If there's a market somewhere for my books, I know she'll find it.

Thanks as well to the warm and open Kate Shewan. I so appreciated the time she took to talk with a stranger about a very delicate subject.

And thanks, I suppose too, should go to the childhood Me. Our situations were very different but there's a lot of little Vicksie Grant in Yardley O'Hanlon. It was fun getting to spend time with her again.